NEW YORK REVIEW BOOKS
CLASSICS

HILL

JEAN GIONO (1895–1970) was born and lived most of his life
in the town of Manosque, Alpes-de-Haute-Provence. Largely
self-educated, he started working as a bank clerk at the age of
sixteen and reported for military service when World War I broke
out. He fought in the battle of Verdun and was one of the few
members of his company to survive. After the war, he returned
to his job and family in Manosque and became a vocal, lifelong
pacifist. After the success of *Hill*, which won the Prix Brentano, he
left the bank and began to publish prolifically. During World War II
Giono's outspoken pacifism led some to accuse him unjustly of
collaboration with the Nazis; after France's liberation in 1944, he
was imprisoned and held without charges. Despite being black-
listed after his release, Giono continued writing and was elected to
the Académie Goncourt in 1954.

PAUL EPRILE is a longtime publisher (Between the Lines,
Toronto), as well as a poet and translator. He is currently at work
on the translation of Jean Giono's novel *Melville* (forthcoming
from NYRB) and lives on the Niagara Escarpment in Ontario,
Canada.

DAVID ABRAM is the director of the Alliance for Wild Ethics.
A cultural ecologist, philosopher, and performance artist, he is the
award-winning author of *Becoming Animal: An Earthly Cosmology* and *The Spell of the Sensuous: Perception and Language in a
More-Than-Human World*. He teaches and lectures around the
world and lives with his family in the foothills of the southern
Rockies.

HILL

JEAN GIONO

Translated from the French by
PAUL EPRILE

Introduction by
DAVID ABRAM

NEW YORK REVIEW BOOKS

New York

THIS IS A NEW YORK REVIEW BOOK
PUBLISHED BY THE NEW YORK REVIEW OF BOOKS
435 Hudson Street, New York, NY 10014
www.nyrb.com

Frontispiece by Claude Boutterin.
First published in French by Bernard Grasset as *Colline*.

Library of Congress Cataloging-in-Publication Data
Names: Giono, Jean, 1895–1970, author. | Eprile, Paul, translator.
Title: Hill / by Jean Giono ; translated by Paul Eprile ; introduction by David
   Abram.
Other titles: Colline. English
Description: New York : New York Review Books, 2016. | Series: New York
   Review Books Classics
Identifiers: LCCN 2015038888 (print) | LCCN 2015046511 (ebook) | ISBN
   9781590179185 (paperback) | ISBN 9781590179192 (epub)
Subjects: | BISAC: FICTION / Literary. | FICTION / Fairy Tales, Folk Tales,
   Legends & Mythology. | FICTION / Psychological.
Classification: LCC PQ2613.I57 C613 2016 (print) | LCC PQ2613.I57 (ebook) |
   DDC 843/.912—dc23
LC record available at http://lccn.loc.gov/2015038888

ISBN 978-1-59017-918-5
Available as an electronic book; ISBN 978-1-59017-919-2

Printed in the United States of America on acid-free paper.
10 9 8 7 6 5 4 3 2 1

CONTENTS

INTRODUCTION

All of man's mistakes arise because he imagines that he walks upon a lifeless thing, whereas his footsteps imprint themselves in a flesh full of vital power.

—JEAN GIONO

THIS TRANSLATION of Jean Giono's *Colline* goes to press during a time of rapidly intensifying ecological disarray. More and more species find themselves plunged into extinction by the steady surge of human progress, while seasonal cycles go haywire and the planet itself shivers into a bone-wrenching fever. Many people find themselves bereft, astonished by the callousness of their own species and by the strange inability of modern civilization to correct its dire course. For those who recognize the animate earth as the source of all sustenance, a future once anticipated with excitement now looms as an inchoate shadow stirring only a vague dread. The disquiet that troubles their sleep stems less from a clear premonition than from the lack of clear images, from the difficulty of glimpsing any way toward a livable world from the place where we are now, at the end—it would seem—of a particular dream of progress.

Where are the fresh ideas, the new forms of perception, the new modes of association that might open us toward a viable future? Yet perhaps the quest for new ideas and new insights—the steady yearning for the *new*—holds us within the same dream of progress that's brought the whole of the biosphere to this uncanny impasse. Instead of always looking off toward the future, perhaps we should strive to become more deeply awake to the full depth of the present moment that surrounds us, opening our eyes and ears to notice the countless other-than-human shapes of sentience that were obscured by the sense-deadening assumptions undergirding the modern era: assumptions regarding the inertness of matter and the mechanical character of material reality, its amenability to being analyzed and figured out by a human mind, or intellect, that floats somehow apart from and above that reality, able to dissociate itself from the body and the bodily earth.

Further, a clear assessment of the current impasse, and the possibilities hidden within it, may best be served by a keen awareness of the many forms of *human* life that were shouldered aside by the march of progress—ways of life we thought were left behind but that still linger (and even flourish) in pockets on the edge of this surging civilization.

The characters in *Hill* inhabit just such a time out of time. High in the foothills of the French Alps, in the shadow of Mount Lure, the inhabitants of a tiny hamlet eke out a tenuous living from a land dense with forests of pine and oak and juniper, thick with rock outcroppings and brambles and the scent of wildflowers (clematis, wormwood, honeysuckle) but also a few small orchards and olive groves, carefully tended. When, in what era? Well, sometime after the invention of the steam-powered threshers working the farms on the plain far below, and the advent of the distant railroad, and yet a long while before the arrival of the automobile: The journey up from the plain takes a full three hours by horse and cart.

These peasants raise a few goats for cheese, and the menfolk hunt whatever they can that's good to eat. Gondran and his wife, Marguerite, Jaume with his drooping mustache and his daughter, Ulalie, the simpleton Gagou and the garrulous but inscrutable elder, Janet—if one said that these were the main characters in the novel, one would not be entirely wrong. But neither would one really be right. For in this work, as in the other early novels of Jean Giono, the primary actors are the elemental powers of the more-than-human earth that enable and necessarily influence all the human happenings. The wind gliding up from the valley and spilling down from the mountain passes is itself a character, as are the flocks of birds who ride the wind's moods, carving their way through its calms and its turbulence, and the forest with its trees heaving and flexing as underground roots feel their way toward fresh moisture. Up above, needles and leaves slowly bask and imbibe the sun's radiance. The shining sun, too, has its exuberant life: "In a single leap the sun clears the crest of the horizon. It enters the sky like a wrestler, atop its undulating arms of fire."

Shaping the tale as well are the creatures who slither and hum and bound within these wooded hills: the wild boar nuzzling among the stones for tubers, swarming insects, snakes coiled in the shade, a feral cat, lizards, hares—all the many sentient lives whose earnest engagements sometimes intersect our human activities at oblique angles (intersections that often go unnoticed, yet now and then catalyze unexpected changes in the habits of a person or the equilibrium of a community). The waters, too, are alive, not just the streams that sometimes swell with fresh rain but also those subterranean flows coursing through interstices in the geological strata, bubbling out of the ground as fresh springs or gushing up through an iron pipe into a carefully crafted fountain. For built things, as well, have their agency—are they not fashioned, after all, from materials birthed by the breathing earth? These whitewashed houses, for example, whose stone walls impart a sense of safety to those who dwell within them—don't these buildings have their own moods and expressions?

> Young Maurras half opens the door of his stable. He looks at the houses one after the other. They're still sleeping, soundlessly, like tired-out animals. Gondran's place alone is making a soft, rattling sound, behind its hedge.... The house has its eyes open—big, watery eyes, which Marguerite's plump shadow passes across like a rolling pupil. The doorway drools a stream of dishwater.

Yet beneath the parched soils, underneath all these many lives, stirs the voluminous life of the hill itself—the brooding body that sustains, supports, and perhaps *feels* all that happens upon its surface. And this hill is but a fold in the broad flesh of Mount Lure, the implacable power spreading its shadowed wings, every evening, over this tiny cluster of houses.

———

Jean Giono was born in 1895, in the rural town of Manosque, a thousand-year-old settlement in the valley of the Durance River, set among the rolling hills, plateaus, and mountains of Alpes-de-Haute-Provence. His mother was a laundress, his father a shoemaker of fiercely independent political and social views. Growing up among the smells of hot irons and steam and freshly washed linen, listening to the sounds of the cobbler's craft making necessary things from simple materials, young Jean gained an early appreciation for the sensuous and palpable textures of life. The sensations gleaned when roaming outside the town walls—watching peasants working the hillside fields, hearing the speech of the scythe and smelling the new-mown wheat, accompanying shepherds as they drive their flocks to the summer pastures high in the mountains (learning the rhythmic and singsong cries by which the herders guide the flocks and signal their sheepdogs)—all such visceral impressions of life lived in direct relation to the seasons settled deep into the young man's memory.

At sixteen he quits school and begins working as a clerk in the local bank to help support his family. He reads Homer in the off-hours. When war breaks out Jean is called up to serve in the infantry, which he does for five years. Posted to the north, he fights in the hellish battle of Verdun—the longest battle of the war. As the armies begin to deploy chemical warfare, his eyelids are scorched by mustard gas in the fighting. He is one of only two members of his company to survive.

The gruesome horror of war, the anguish of watching so many comrades die, scarred Giono's soul. The sheer insanity of it, the inconceivable waste of life by the newly mechanized forms of warfare, each side racing to overcome the other with more effective killing machines—machine guns, armored tanks, tanks with rotating turrets, flamethrowers, poison gas, fighter airplanes, bombers—transformed Giono into an ardent pacifist, with a distaste verging on disgust for so-called "progress." He made his way back home, past forests now leveled to stumps, past long-cultivated fields turned to muck and farm animals starved and dying. In Manosque, with most of his generation dead or wounded, he took up again his job at the bank, married, started a family, and soon began to write, exploring with words the possibility of other ways of living, other ways of feeling and thinking that might draw humankind in a different direction, that might induce a swerve in our collective trajectory, away from the growing mechanization of life and the inevitability of further war. He began to write of the *earth*—of a living relation to the elemental, earthly cosmos as the necessary source of all human solidarity, as the inescapable (but easily overlooked) ground of all affection between persons and between cultures, as the very possibility of peace.

———

Hill was Giono's first published novel (he ultimately published more than fifty books, the great majority of which were works of fiction), and in this work we find him grappling with and giving a first shape to themes that would remain central to all his early novels, and in some manner to all his life's work. Giono's vision is intensely—even overwhelmingly—ecological. I say "overwhelmingly" because this vision is glimpsed by the human protagonists in *Hill* only in moments of epiphany, when it threatens to swamp all their settled assumptions regarding the workings of the world. In part this indirection is due to Giono's greatness as a novelist: He will never spell everything out for his readers but will afford us only partial and fragmentary glimpses of a mystery that resists any total understanding. Yet it's also a result of Giono's own exploratory moves toward a stance that remains somewhat embryonic in this first work but will gradually emerge as a full-blown animate cosmology (though again, never spelled out: a cosmos that can only be sensed from one's limited position within its depths) in *Song of the World*, published five years later. In that work, the human figures are fully a part of the wild and darkly breathing cosmos (indeed, the two human protagonists seem to be walking expressions of the river and the forest, respectively), while in *Hill* the human characters are negotiating their first, dawning awareness of their inherence within a world that is, itself, alive . . . and the prospect terrifies them.

Although the coarse and spiteful elder, Janet, carries something of this cosmological vision as a secret within his now-paralyzed body, it's his son-in-law, Gondran, who first stumbles upon this strange new angle of sight while hoeing in his olive grove. He's feeling strong; it's a fine day, and when his spade startles a lizard that darts out from under the grass, Gondran can't resist the sudden intoxication of power: He slashes the reptile with his spade and watches its severed limbs writhe in the dirt. But then, upon noticing the creature's blood, an unease quietly comes over him, stopping up his throat like a stone. "While he digs, it occurs to him for the first time that there's a kind of blood rising inside bark, just like his own blood; that a fierce will to live makes the tree branches twist and propels these sprays of grasses into the sky."

Sensing for the first time the life stirring all around him in plants, in animals, he begins to wonder at the suffering that he unleashes when he scythes or when he cuts down a tree. The epiphany grows: Perhaps even the stones are alive, and the rocky ground where he stands. "This earth! . . . what if she really is a living being, what if she really is one body?"

The vision swells, intensifies, transforms everything around him: "An immense life force, slow to move, but awesome in its naked power, rouses the stupendous body of earth, flows over her valleys and knolls, folds her flatlands, bends her rivers, and builds up her thick coat of soil and vegetation."

Yet Gondran, the simple peasant, cannot contain this vision; what it straightaway stirs in him is fear, terror. What if this living earth has bad intentions? What if its massive body is readying itself to destroy him, the way he slashed that lizard? "In no time, to avenge herself, she'll haul me up to where the skylarks lose their breath."

He rushes back to the houses to warn the others. Over a bottle of absinthe (a recipe perfected by old Janet) the other men ponder the ramifications, taking care not to alarm the women. The most reflective of them, Jaume, only amplifies Gondran's concern, spreading his paranoia to the others. They arm themselves; they become watchful, on the lookout for . . . what? They do not know. Only that something in this broad terrain may be out to get them for the way they've been treating the land. Perhaps the hill itself.

——

It might be worth pointing out that the author did not title his novel *La Colline* (The Hill) but rather *Colline* (*Hill*). Given that nouns, in French, are pretty much *always* preceded by a definite or indefinite article, the fact that here *Hill* stands on its own seems significant. Indeed atop Giono's manuscript, he had written "La Colline," but then had crossed out the definite article. Perhaps the reason lies here: When we use a definite or indefinite article in front of any noun—a bear, the bear—it entails a slight distance from that being, either for classification (as one bear among many) or specification (the bear, there). But when we dispense with an article and speak of this presence as Bear, there is no distance. The object involves us totally. "The Hill" determines a particular hill that we may approach or envision from a distance. Hill names a power that absorbs us, and may even, perhaps, subsume us.

——

Giono spoke of this work, and the two novels that shortly followed it—*Un de Baumugnes* in 1929 (published in English as *Lovers Are Never Losers*) and *Regain* in 1930 (published in English as *Second Harvest*)—as his Pan trilogy, although the three stories are not connected. Nor is the god Pan overtly mentioned in any of them. Yet in these first novels the author hoped to invoke the rich energies associated with this deity, and to impart something of that wild magic to those who read the work. Half human in visage, but with the horns and hindquarters of a goat, Pan is the god of untamed places, of woodlands and meadows and reedy swamps, the spirit of deep forests and high rocky slopes that only mountain goats can navigate. An ally of all things wild, the horned god is the hair-raising power that moves in the depths of nature; he's the lilt in rustic music and the sexual abandon of springtime—the spontaneity and robust exuberance of renewal. For some, Pan is but one of several names of a horned personification of the wild that was honored in many parts of pre-Christian Europe but was later demonized by the church, transformed into the cloven-hooved and horned image of the Devil.

As is evident from the eight or nine novels that followed *Hill*, Giono was preparing to invoke the vitalizing aspect of Pan in his writings, the creative and regenerative exuberance that the god can instill in those who've learned to align themselves with the cycles of wild nature. But with this first novel he wanted to present the more unsettling and dangerous quality of this power, that which can unnerve persons who stumble inadvertently into wild terrain, inducing a headlong fear that's come to be called "panic" since it's provoked by Pan's proximity.

Such is the state toward which our peasant farmers begin to slide upon hearing Gondran's visionary perception that everything around them is alive. Their disquiet deepens when the fountain—their sole source of water—suddenly stops flowing, as though its throat were plugged up. As their thirst grows and their fear intensifies, the relations between them get more jagged; things are coming unglued. All that the men can think of is to consult the foul-tempered Janet, who lies paralyzed and dying on his mattress, hallucinating snakes and rehearsing obscene memories. Jaume decides to brave the old man's scorn. He lays out their situation for Janet—who after all is the only one among them who understood how to douse for water or to divine the weather, a gnarled tree of an old man who alone knew the arcane uses of all the plants thereabouts. Janet listens but only stalls at first, goading Jaume with insults, until, breathing hard, he slips into a treelike trance, and his earthen voice comes unblocked—as though the stopped-up waters of the fountain had found this new outlet. The torrent of speech tells of uncanny powers ... of a strange landlord in a sheepskin coat whose voice is the sighing of the wind, a master of tenderness who speaks to foxes, hawks, and chestnut trees all in their own tongue.

Jaume listens, tries to take it all in. Yet he can no more integrate this weird knowledge than Gondran can his earlier vision. It's too ambiguous, too complex, too difficult to reconcile. Old Janet must be tricking him. Something evil, he suspects, must be at work, and Janet—in cahoots with the rocks, the wild boars, and the surging mass of green life—is probably behind it.

———

For those reared in a Christian culture (even rustic and relatively impious peasants) the first contact with Pan stirs fear, brings panic. Vouched even a faint glimpse into the horned god's polyerotic cosmos, wherein plants are sentient and the wind is alive, the immediate impulse is to try to assimilate that wild vision to one's habitual sense of morality, which sorts things into those that are *good* and those that are *bad*. Yet the multiform and shadowed richness of the wild, wherein each being—trout, sycamore, mountain lion—enacts its own interplay with the local earth while being dependent upon all the others, can never be squared with such a black-and-white logic. The radical *plurality* of willful organisms and elements acting seemingly at cross-purposes within any mostly wild ecosystem necessarily confounds any simple polarity between a pure good and a pure evil. Faced with wild nature's unruly refusal to sort itself into two camps, civilization cannot help but demonize it—construing nature as a malevolent realm that must be subdued, blunted, and brought under control.

Giono was too awake, and too savvy an artist, to present a bucolic view of nature shorn of its ferocity and bloodletting, stripped of its capricious moods and its manifest dangers. Yet he knew well the inner conflict that his nascent ecological stance would stir within his fellow citizens, the impossibility of reconciling such a stance with a collective worldview based upon the denigration of the senses by the intellect and the subjugation of nature by technology. He knew the instinctive recourse to conventional moral categories that the vision of an animate, breathing planet would provoke...because the same conflict was roiling in his own chest. It roils in us, too, as we keep reading: Is old Janet simply a *scapegoat* upon whom the other characters project their fears? Or is he an avatar of that *other* goat, the capricious goat god himself, able to rally the malevolence of nature with his witching language? By letting this unresolved tension unfurl among the several characters in *Hill*, Giono was clearing out his conscience and his creativity for the full espousal of the pagan, animist cosmos that his subsequent fiction would undertake—for the massively erotic, earthly faith that was soon to burst upon his readers.

———

Giono's insights into the consequences of a way of life that elevates itself above the rest of nature, and his insights regarding the contours of a truly ecological culture, hold vital clues for our contemporary situation. His early novels call us toward the primacy of *place*, and the importance of bodily engagement with the creatures and the seasons of a place. They encourage a renewal of small-scale, face-to-face community, and stress that no human community can be healthy without honoring its thorough embedment within a wider, more-than-human community of animals, plants, and earthly elements. For Giono was convinced that our social bonds inevitably fray and falter if they're not fed by interaction with the living land; that the best chance for a just society, and the only prospect for a meaningful peace, lies in renouncing the dream of mastery and dedicating ourselves—wherever we find ourselves—to the replenishment and flourishing of the local earth.*

More significantly, Giono realizes that we'll continue to hold ourselves aloof from the rest of nature as long as we assume that subjectivity is an exclusively human possession, or even that the capacity for feelingful experience is reserved solely for those beings that are deemed "alive" by the natural sciences. Only by reconceiving life as a quality proper to the whole of this earthly cosmos do we free our bodily senses to engage, to participate, to resonate with every aspect of the sensuous surroundings. When we concede that mountains and rivers have their own forms of vitality, that the ground itself senses our weight, that the winds and the thunderclouds seethe with sensation and feeling—only then do we free our own sentience to find its place within the wider matrix.

With this notion, Giono taps into a logic much older than the literate intellect, with its capacity for detachment and abstraction. The deeply animistic way of speaking that he deploys in his novels of peasant life is common to nonliterate, oral cultures throughout the world and is especially pronounced among indigenous, place-based peoples. Such discourse is also preserved in a tradition closer to the author's Mediterranean heritage, the Greek epics of Homer (who was himself an oral rhapsode, a nonliterate bard). Just as Homer draws steadily upon a stock of repeated epithets—"the wine-dark sea," "rosy-fingered dawn"—so Giono has his own stock of similes and metaphoric phrases that return again and again in these novels, although always with a freshness that makes the phrase seem newly born: the wind speaks with a thousand green tongues; the rain walks across the land; one's inward mood buzzes like a swarm of

---

*For those readers who wish to sample Giono's ecological cosmology in its full wonder, I suggest reading, at minimum, *Song of the World* (1934), translated by Henri Fluchere and Geoffrey Myers, and *Joy of Man's Desiring* (1935), translated by Katherine Allen Clarke, as well as Giono's well-known fable, *The Man Who Planted Trees* (especially as brought to the screen by the artist Frédéric Back, whose animated film won an Oscar in 1988).

bees; the sun leaps into the sky neighing like a stallion (in *Song of the World*), or leaps into the sky bristling like a wrestler (in *Hill*).

Indeed, throughout his first ten novels Giono seems intent on celebrating and rejuvenating oral culture—the culture of convivial storytelling, of spontaneous oral eloquence, of musical speech and word magic. Not to the exclusion of literate culture (Giono was a prodigious lover of literature) but rather *underneath* the culture of books: He wanted to replenish this more ancient, visceral layer of language that holds our ears open to the speech of rivers and woodlands and the rain.

And it's here, I believe, that we find Giono's most remarkable contribution to the work of cultural metamorphosis, and to the prospect of an ecological future. In contrast to those who contend that verbal language, by its nature, necessarily breaks our direct, present-moment experience of the world around us—that the simple act of speaking inevitably tears the speaker out of her felt, sensorial participation with the sensuous surroundings—Giono shows that there exist ways of speaking that actually *open* our senses, ways of wielding words that can hold our speaking bodies in attentive rapport with the more-than-human terrain. He was the great pioneer of such a language, discovering an array of oral techniques that can be applied and put to use in our own time.

For example: Giono often elucidates human events by way of metaphors drawn directly from the local earth, while describing shifts in the surrounding landscape using metaphors drawn from the human body (or from the physical gestures of other animals). While today it has become a facile commonplace to say "the earth is alive," the meaning becomes far more compelling when we speak of the visible terrain as *flesh*—as a living, breathing *body*. Moreover, it is one thing to be *intellectually* convinced of our human interdependence with other beings; Giono showed that by using corporeal and sensorial turns of phrase that mingle the flesh of humans and other animals with that of plants and earthly elements; by wielding metaphors that merge weather phenomena with sensations that we feel in our torso or our limbs; by combining in one extended metaphor terms drawn from different sensory modalities (that is, by using audible terms to describe visual phenomena, or tactile terms to describe olfactory sensations)—such intellectual notions begin to be experienced as visceral, felt realities.

We will not likely mobilize others to act on behalf of a more-than-human earth if our everyday language holds us aloof from that earth—if even the discourse of environmentalism remains couched in mechanical and statistical terms that stifle any instinctive, animal empathy with the animate terrain. The American philosopher Richard Rorty held that it is not those persons who *argue well* who are likely to change the world, but rather those who *speak differently.* For all who work for ecological change, and for a societal swerve away from our currently calamitous trajectory, Jean Giono remains the great artist of such a way of speaking differently.

—DAVID ABRAM

HILL

To the memory of my father.
—Jean Giono

To the memory of my father.
—P. E.

FOUR HOUSES, orchids flowering up to the eaves, emerge from a dense stand of grain.

Up there among the hills, where earth's flesh folds in thick rolls.

Sainfoin in bloom bleeds red under the olive trees. Bees dance around birches sticky with sap.

A fountain murmurs and overflows in two streams that plunge from a ledge and scatter in the wind. Gurgling under the grass, they reunite and course through a bed of rushes.

The wind hums in the plane trees.

These are the Bastides Blanches, the White Houses.

The remnants of a hamlet perched halfway between the plain, where steam-powered threshers roar in tumult, and the vast, lavender wasteland, the wind's domain, in the frigid shadow of the mountain range of Lure.

The land of wind.

And the land of the untamed too: the garter snake coils from a spray of lavender; the squirrel darts, canopied by its tail, clutching an acorn; the weasel jabs its snout into the wind, a bead of blood glistening on its whisker tip; the fox reads the tracks of the partridge through the grass.

The wild boar groans under the junipers. Her babies, milk trickling from their mouths, prick their ears at the tall, gesticulating trees.

Then the wind lets go of the trees, silence lulls the branches, and the litter of the grunting sow snort as they tug at her teats.

Wild things and people from the Bastides cross paths at the spring, this fluid running out of solid rock, so soothing to both tongue and coat.

After nightfall in the open country there's a muffled migration toward anything that's singing and fresh.

And by daylight too, when thirst becomes overwhelming.

The solitary wild boar sniffs his way toward the farmsteads.

He knows all about siesta time.

At a trot he makes a wide detour under cover of the shrubs. Then, from the nearest point, he leaps.

And now he's in deep. He wallows in the water. Mud coats his belly.

Freshness envelops him head to tail, back to belly.

He bites at the mouth of the spring.

Sweet, liquid coolness laps against his skin.

All of a sudden he tears himself away from these transports of pleasure and gallops off toward the woods.

He's heard a farmhouse shutter squeak.

He's well aware that a shutter tends to squeak when someone tries to open it carefully.

Jaume fires a round of buckshot, blind.

A leaf drops from the linden.

"What did you fire at?"

"A boar. Look at it over there, the son of a whore."

Calm, blue, Mount Lure dominates the landscape and blocks out the west with its huge, numb, mountain body.

Gray vultures haunt it.

They wheel all day in the watery sky like sage leaves.

Sometimes they take off on voyages.

Other times they sleep with their wings spread, breasting the steady force of the breeze.

Then Lure looms up between earth and sun, and long before nightfall its shadow plunges the Bastides into darkness.

Married couples live in two of the houses.

One belongs to Gondran le Médéric. He married Marguerite Ricard. Her father, Janet, lives with them.

One belongs to Aphrodis Arbaud. He married a woman from Pertuis.

They have two little daughters, one three, one five.

Then there are:

César Maurras, his mother, and their young welfare worker.

Alexandre Jaume, who lives with his daughter, Ulalie. And finally, Gagou.

So they're an even dozen, plus Gagou, who throws off the reckoning.

The houses enclose a small square of bare ground—a shared space, and a place for playing at *boules*.

The wash house lies under the big oak.

You scrub your laundry in a sandstone sarcophagus carved on the inside to resemble a man in chain mail.

The cavity for the cadaver brims with green, brackish water that quivers with the etchings of aquatic insects.

The sides of this massive coffin hold images of women flagellating themselves with laurel boughs.

Aphrodis Arbaud unearthed this age-old stone one time when he was uprooting an olive tree.

The houses mirror their occupants.

A bushy Virginia creeper climbs all over Jaume's place, and above the front door it looks just like the walrus moustache that hangs over his mouth.

And they're all like that.

Arbaud's: dolled up and painted with ochre twice a year; Gondran's place, Maurras's place, and Gagou's.

Oh yes, Gagou's place resembles its owner too.

He arrived at the Bastides on a summer's evening three years ago, just when they were finished winnowing late-ripened wheat with the night wind.

A piece of string held up his britches; he was shirtless.

A drooping lip, a lifeless eye, but blue, blue ... and two buck teeth sticking out through his lips.

He drooled.

People asked him questions. He answered only: "Gagou, ga ... gou ..." on two different notes, like some sort of animal.

Then he danced the way marmots do, swaying, and dangling his hands.

A simpleton.

They gave him a meal, and some straw to bed down on.

The Bastides had once been a market town, back in the days when the seigneurs of Aix liked to breathe the bracing air of the hills.

All of their fine houses have crumbled to dust. Only the peasants' remain standing.

Even so, on the far side of the wash house two grass-covered pillars mark the entrance to a lane.

Pillars capped by globes with hoods of moss and Latin inscriptions.

Over there, an iron gate must have blocked the entrance to what they called a folly.

Balconies like the wombs of goddesses ... terraces with the swish of a skirt and the click of high heels.

Right in the middle of the space between the pillars, and four yards back, Gagou has erected his shack, in the thick of the nettles.

He's industrious, and surprisingly clever with his hands. He's built his hut out of corrugated iron and flattened fuel cans.

Now that he's cleared the grass from the feet of the pillars, you can make out a high-sounding name engraved inside a laurel-crowned cartouche.

It's a long way to town, and the roads are rough.

When the wind blows from the south you can hear trains whistling and bells ringing down below.

Which, up here, means only that it's going to rain.

When the heat haze disperses, from town you can spot the Bastides perched like doves on the hill's shoulder.

Last year the postman came up a lot. Almost once a week. Young Maurras was doing his military service in the dragoons.

Now that he's back he doesn't have to write home anymore. He just has to shout from the square or from the fields, and his mother comes out and asks, "What do you want?"

So the postman has stopped coming.

Except for every once in a while at the end of the month, when the loans they've taken out with the notary fall due.

Which amounts to saying that they'd rather not see him at all.

Whatever comes from town is bad: the wind that brings rainy weather, and the postman.

Nobody would disagree.

They prefer the wind that blows from the wasteland of Lure. It cuts like a razor, but it scatters the magpies and it points the way, for those in the know, to where the hares hide.

Gondran's house is the last one facing the plain. It's called Les Monges—maybe because it's on its own and robed in red like a monk; maybe because once upon a time it really was a hermitage. All in all, it has the look of a grand old priest's house, with its stout buttresses and its low-set, curve-topped door; the house of one of those halfwhoremonger priests who happily give a meal and a bed to lovers stealing away to make love in peace.

It's the best situated of the four. It guards the road and has a view of the hill. It's right beside the slope that runs down to the lowlands. From the terrace you can make out the switchbacks all the way down to La Clémente.

At one time Les Monges belonged to Janet, the oldest resident of the Bastides. Janet has lived here since he was thirty. He moved up after he'd done a stint on every farm down on the plain. Nobody wanted to hire him anymore, because he fought with all the other hands. Three times a week they'd have to send for the gendarmes and break out the sticking plasters. His wife died here; his daughter grew up here. Now he's in his eighties. He's straight-limbed, tough as a laurel trunk, and his thin lips barely crease the sculpted boxwood of his face. From his beady, chestnut-coloured eyes his blank stare flits into the sky like a moth. That's where he divines the weather and knows when trees will come into leaf. That's where he predicts sickness, sees faces. And that's where he detects, he of all people—supreme liar and trickster—lying and treachery. He's never left the Bastides, but you don't say "Janet's place" anymore. You say "Gondran's place." Gondran is his son-in-law. Janet has had to go along with all of this. You say: "Gondran's house, Gondran's fields. The horse, the cart, the hay—they're all Gondran's." Gondran has entirely taken over from Janet. Gondran is broad across the shoulders, tall, rosy-cheeked. The plough runs true in his hands. Once, he tamed an unruly mule with a single blow to its ear.

Deep down, Janet does hold something against Gondran. He begrudges him mainly because of his daughter. It's because of her, after all, that Gondran has taken over his place.

Since then, to his way of thinking, she's done nothing worthwhile.

"Back in my day, they knew how to make real bean soup."

"The hare is good, but you've put ten times too much water in the sauce."

He'd be happy to see her beaten.

"If I were you," he says to his son-in-law, "I'd tan her hide."

"Bloody well right!" Gondran replies, with a laugh.

Stout Marguerite trots in on her stubby legs and, putting on a pout, raises her eyebrows good-naturedly: "There you go, papa, you're never satisfied."

Today Gondran steps out onto the terrace. In one hand he holds a bottle and two glasses. With the other arm he cradles a clay pitcher full of fresh water that's trickling all the way down into his pants. He shifts the table with his foot, sets down the jug and the glasses, and then, with great care, the bottle.

Six o'clock on a summer's evening. They're singing over at the wash house.

With his arms swinging he stretches twice. Spade work has bent his stocky frame. At the end of the second stretch, he farts. It's his ritual.

He sits down, drags a glass across the table. He holds the bottle up against the daylight. It's half full of greenish liquor, and at the bottom there's a mat of herbs, leaves, and tiny brown seeds. This is an absinthe he makes at home with artemisia from the hills, aniseed that he orders from the postman, and his own aged eau de vie.

Drop by drop he adds the water. He's gripped the jug by the neck in his hefty, dirt-caked hand and he holds it effortlessly, tilted above his glass.

Two puffs on his pipe, then the still air carries him a hint of a sound.

He leans over, and stares at the bend in the road at Les Ponches, down there among the hawthorns. That's where he'll be able to see it the best.

Now he's spotted it.

"Gritte, he's here!" he shouts toward the kitchen.

It's a cabriolet that's climbing. Swaying in the ruts like a stout little cargo boat. The nag is ringing its bell.

Maurras passes by, dragging some bundles of olive branches.

"César, come over and have a glass."

"Pour me one. I'm going to feed the goats. I'll be right back."

By now the horse's bell is ringing just behind the embankment. At last the carriage appears. It slides into the little square, like a snail. The horse knows how to take care of itself—it goes on its own to the watering trough. The man makes his way up to Gondran's.

As he steps on to the terrace, he says in astonishment, "Hey, what's that you're drinking?" Then, right away, "Come on, let me have a little."

There is an empty glass sitting there waiting for him, after all. Before he arrived, Gondran had winked to César, "Wait and see how he knocks it back."

It's the doctor. Reddish hair and blue eyes. His left eyebrow, exaggeratedly long and pointed, sticks out of his forehead like a little horn. His broad, hairy hands are covered with freckles.

"Here's to your health."

He drinks, wipes his wickerwork moustache, and says, "Well, then, what seems to be the matter?"

Gondran pushes away his glass and coughs. Once. He coughs again. He draws his glass back, leans on his elbows, and says, at long last, "It's my father-in-law. He came down with it the other night when we were watering the meadow. I'd sent him to the far end to shout out when the water got there. I was keeping an eye on the sluice. I knew he'd gone back to the house for a few nips—I could see him going back and forth in the moonlight. But then, for a long time he didn't move.

"I shouted: 'Janet! Hey, Janet!' Nothing. No answer. At first I didn't think much about it. I know him. He'll lie down in the grass, and right until the water tickles his nose he won't wake up. It's his way. I've told him a hundred times: 'One of these days you'll drown.' Which, now you can see, did him about as much good as . . .

"So, no answer. I was thinking: 'Whatever, it's incredible the water isn't there yet.' But with all those bloody mole-holes you never know. So I busted open the main channel with my spade.

"The water rushed out. It was making the grass on the banks hiss like the wind. A minute later I called out again. Nothing. Now this was beginning to get rather peculiar. So I go down and look around. I didn't have a lantern. To tell you the truth—I was scared. What if I found him dead? At his age.

"He was stretched out on the ground, stiff. The water was up to an inch from his mouth. To get him out of there wasn't easy, believe me. I was buried up to my knees in mud.

"We put him into his bed. And afterward he ate, he drank, he chewed his wad of tobacco, he talked, he could move his fingers and the lower parts of his arms. But the rest of him is as dead as a tree trunk.

"So, go take a peek at him."

"That's why I've come."

The doctor savors the rest of his drink in little sips, smoothes out the horn of his eyebrow, then goes into the kitchen, where Marguerite's tuneless voice immediately kicks up a fuss.

"Another shot, César?"

"Another shot."

The doctor comes out.

"So?"

"He's old. What age exactly?"

"In his eighties."

"When you're that far along, there isn't really any more medicine you can take. Purge him. Give him whatever he wants. I don't think he has much time left. He'd had a bit to drink, eh?"

Gondran smiles. He glances at César, then at the doctor.

"A bit? Papa Janet? Maybe he wasn't a champion drinker, but he did knock back his six litres every day. I'm only talking about the wine, eh, I'm not counting the eau de vie—that's something else, or the bubbly, or the rosé, or the cherries in brandy—the night he got sick he'd sucked back half a jarful."

"All this comes out in the wash, in the end. I don't believe he has much time left. But with a carcass like his, anything's possible. Do what I told you. However, in my opinion, it's like putting a bandage on a wooden leg. If he gets any worse, come and get me if you want, but it is a long way. It took me three hours to get up here."

Night is already pouring into the valley. It washes over the haunch of the hill. The olive groves raise their song, under the shadow.

Gondran accompanies the doctor to his cabriolet and holds the horse by its bit.

"See you, Doctor."

"See you. Don't forget to purge him. He may have a bit of delirium. With alcoholics you always have to be ready for it. Don't let it scare you."

With the first squeak of the wheels he changes his mind:

"You know what—there's no point getting me to come back. It's going to run its natural course. There's nothing to be done about it.

"You don't know if you can take a carriage through the Garidelles shortcut, do you?"

"Sometimes they hang on longer than you could possibly believe," says César. "Look at Papa Burle. It got the better of him last summer, but he lasted all winter and another summer, and oh my goodness, did he ever stink in the heat. We had to change him three times a day. He had worms right up his crack."

To begin with, they laid him down in his own bedroom, but he called out a hundred times a day for his daughter, Marguerite, with a pleading voice like a little girl hailing her goats.

First to uncover his feet, then to lift up his head, then he's hungry, then he's thirsty. Then he wants his plug, and Marguerite slices the tobacco with her sewing scissors.

There are three steps leading up to his bedroom, and Marguerite's feet are swollen from all the to-ing and fro-ing.

"What if we set his bed up in the kitchen? It would be a lot better, and I wouldn't get so worn out."

Finally they set it up next to the fireplace. If he leans over the edge, he can catch a glimpse of his daughter getting supper ready over the fire pit, where a spiteful-looking eye glows from the embers.

And he talks.

Nonstop, like a fountain, like an underground stream springing out from the very core of a mountain.

"...the Mane fair was the best by far for the whores from the whole district. There was a guy named Lance who got us all betting on numbered balls. If you didn't choose the right one, you'd end up having to do it in the hayloft.

"...at the first inn on the right I always used to eat onion soup. You know, like clockwork. I'd arrive at Volx at dawn. I'd hammer on the door with my brake rod. The lady of the house would open the window. 'Is it you, Janet?' She knew my knock. She'd come down in her chemise to let me in, I'd give her a little squeeze on the ass, and the rest would take care of itself....

"...he was in there, huddled up in the straw against the grain bin, with his back arched like a cat. I knew he had his crook with him. 'Is it you, you old bugger?' I asked him. 'It's me,' he said, 'and what the hell, is it against the law now to take a nap in your own house?' So I grabbed the pitchfork. 'I'll show you, you'll see...'"

He laughs, softly, and then his steely eye turns toward the cauldrons: "Gritte, my bean soup, is it for tomorrow, or for today?"

This evening Marguerite hasn't had time to cook. Gondran is eating a raw onion for supper. He's sliced it down the middle. One by one he peels the concentric layers, dips them in the salt cellar, and downs them.

It's a sickly kind of evening. The wind has picked up from the Rhône. A storm must be blocking the Mondragon gorge.

All day long the river of wind has been sweeping through the Drôme basin. When it reached as high as the chestnut groves, it blew through the big branches to beat the devil. It swelled out little by little till it flooded over the mountains. And then, having crossed that brink, it roared down right on top of us, wreathed with bunches of leaves.

Now it's whistling around the Bastides, through the fluted chambers hollowed out in the rock by primordial torrents.

The woods are dancing. Shreds of storm flit by. A sharp bolt rumbles and flashes. The air bears scents of sulphur, gravel, and ice. A liquid light tints the windowpane, where an ivy that's come away from the wall is banging its arm, laden with leaves.

The attic door jumps on its hinges. You'd think somebody was stomping out an unwanted litter of kittens up there. Night is thickening. The wind is starting to yowl. The sky resounds like corrugated metal in a hailstorm.

A long moan travels the length of the house. It can't be the skylight—it's fastened down. The window? It's rattling, but it's not moaning. And the bolt is new.

So what can it be?

Gondran eats. The onion crunches between his teeth. Which prevents him from really hearing the moaning that's intriguing him. So he stops chewing.

The moaning is coming to life. It's bearing its own piercing body from the flesh of the shivering house.

Janet is stretched out under the sheets, stiff and straight. His slender body lifts the gray blanket into a furrow-mound. Bird's breath flutters across his chest. You might even say that it looks like a seed wanting to break through its casing and unfurl its leaves into the sunlight. This is what Gondran imagines as he munches his onion.

Janet has a forbidding air this evening: skin blue as granite, hardened nose bones, nostrils translucent like flints. Out of the shadow, his one open eye glints with the glimmer of stone, like one of those outcrops hidden deep in the ground, which a big, polished ploughshare, one that usually runs true, will buckle up against and flip over.

"What if this lasts all summer and all winter, like it did with Papa Burle?"

You'd think Janet was moving his fingers. Now what's he up to?

With difficulty, he's uncovered his hands. He's spread them out on the sheet. He looks at them with his one open eye, which, gradually, widens in a stupor. His right hand moves slowly toward his left hand.

It's the movement of a growing branch, the movement of a plant.

His right hand seizes his left, squeezes it, stretches it out. It looks as if it's trying to pull off a glove or some kind of binding. Next, slowly, ponderously, as though inflated with appalling force, but still having to strain to lift an enormous weight, the hand advances toward the edge of the bed and makes a throwing motion. And then it begins again, always the same, like a machine.

Gondran moves nearer. From here, closer up, he can see the veins quivering in Janet's hand. They're like the ropes they use to tie up baby goats.

"Papa Janet, what are you doing?"

Janet is as stiff as a wooden saint. He draws his marble pupil into the corner of his eye.

"The snakes," he says. "The snakes."

"What snakes?"

"The snakes, I'm telling you. The ones in my fingers. I have snakes in my fingers. I can feel their scales scraping inside."

He chuckles, like a pine nut crackles when you crush it.

"I'm on the lookout for them. When a head sticks out from under one of my nails I grab it, I yank on it, the whole stinking vermin comes out, and then I toss it on the ground. Meanwhile, another one comes up through my finger. I pull it out and I toss it down too. It's a tiresome job, but when my hands are clear of them I won't feel so rotten anymore."

Gondran, flabbergasted, looks at Janet, then at the bedside rug. Nothing there—just red and blue flowers.

"You're raving," he says.

"I'm raving? Look..."

The action begins again, slow, methodical. Janet wants to prove it. His clenched fist stretches out from the side of the bed, opens up... His pupil gleams victoriously from the corner of his eye.

Gondran has seen nothing. And now he's a bit more sure of himself.

"You're raving, I tell you. You're sick in the head. There aren't any snakes in your hands. There aren't any there on the ground. If there were any snakes, I'd see them. I'd see them," he repeats, scraping the thick soles of his shoes across the bare tiles.

The shutter leaps; the ivy beats against the windowpane. The moaning descends from the attic, plunges into the thick air of the room below, cleaves through the odor of onions, cold ashes, and sweat, and vanishes under the vibrating door.

"I'm 'raving.' And who do you think you are, to say I'm 'raving'?"

Janet is talking to the shadows, to no one in particular, and couldn't care less about Gondran, who's watching him intently and drinking up his weird words.

"So you think you see everything, do you, with your pathetic eyes? Can you see the wind too, you with your tremendous powers?

"When you come right down to it, you're incapable of looking at a tree and seeing anything but a tree.

"People like you believe trees are dropped straight into the ground, with their leaves and all, and that's the end of it, right there. Oh boy, if only it were so, it would be so easy.

"You don't see anything there, under the chair?

"Nothing but air?

"Do you really believe it's empty, the air?

"Come on now, you really believe the air's completely empty?

"Well then, look—there's a house over there, a tree, and a hill, and you really think everything around them is just empty? You believe the house is a house and nothing more? The hill, just a hill and nothing more than that?

"I didn't know you were such a useless bugger.

"There, under the chair, just a second ago, I tossed three of them. One was a teeny green one, a grass snake. He looked like he had three braided oat stalks on his back. I have no idea why, but when he flipped out of my finger, he called out 'Hey, Auguste!' My name isn't Auguste. My name's Janet.

"There was another one, thick, and short, the kind we call an ass's prick, and another one that was whistling music that sounded like it was coming from a mouth organ. That one was a female. The skin on her belly was swollen. She's going to have babies. She had a hard time, that one, squeezing out of my finger.

"Look, look quick now, there's one climbing up the side of the cauldron to get at the milk. Big bubbles of milk are sliding down its gullet.

"You don't see it?

"So then, do you still think the air's empty?

"If you had them inside your fingers, like I have, you'd know.

"If you'd ever come face to face all at once, one evening, with what's in the air down at the bend in the road, you'd see them like I do.

"The hill. You'll notice it one day from the hill.

"For the time being our hill's lying down like an ox in the grass, and only its back is showing. Ants are crawling all over its bristles, running back and forth.

"For the moment it's lying down, but if it ever gets up, then you'll tell me whether I'm raving or not...

"Look, look at that one! A real beauty with eyes like apples. Oh, but that one, he has eyes like a man. He's tearing at my flesh. Ayay, ay me!

"And then there's that one, the one over there on the floor. It's twisting itself up tighter than a worm that's cut in two. Look at it there pretending to be dying, the sly devil ..."

Gondran looks right and left: the tiles are bare.

But Janet's still making out that the bedside rug is moving. Under the table, there's one of them! Under the table—a snake as thick as your thumb, sleeping, curled into the shape of an *S*.

"It's the lash of a whip."

"It's a snake."

"It's the lash of a whip."

Outside, the weight of the wind is crushing the oak. Dead branches crash into the watering trough. The chimney begins to roar, and ashes swirl around the fireplace like the dust stirred up by a flock of sheep.

In two bounds Gondran is at the door. It takes all his strength to wrench it open—the bolt is jammed so hard into the wall—and he bawls out toward the goat barn, where Marguerite is sorting some olive boughs:

"Gritte? Gritte? Aren't you done down there yet, goddamit?"

The wind's blown for two days and two nights, loaded with clouds. Now it's raining. The storm that the gorge had blocked has reared up like a bull lashed by grass blades. It's ripped itself out of the mud of the plains. First, its muscular back expanded, then it leapt over the hills and charged off across the sky.

It's raining. A little raging rain, stirred up and then appeased for no reason, pierced by arrows of sunlight, battered by the rough blows of the wind, but undaunted. And its eager feet have flattened the oats. The entire population of swallows and blackbirds is sounding off in the trees.

The sky is like a swamp where patches of open water gleam between pools of slime.

At first Jaume had set himself down under the oak to sharpen his scythe. The leaves were shading him. He laughed at the women racing to bring the laundry in from the line. But the rain chased him off, just like the others. And now the folded sack he's been sitting on is soaked like a sponge.

Arbaud, standing in the doorway of his barn, watches the rain. He's been meaning to head off to the hill. Now he's unhitched his mule. Maurras and Jaume have come to meet up with him.

The rain.

The fountain murmurs in unison, under the tree.

Gondran has turned up too, with his back arched against the downpour.

"Shitty weather!"

"Every time I'm set to go and make hay, it's the same thing."

Gondran's talking. He's been mulling his words over and over, he's cursed the weather, he's said what there is to say about the rain and the shape the soil is in, but now he's striking at the root.

"I tell you, in my whole lifetime I've never seen anything remotely like this. I have to wonder where on earth he gets his crazy ideas. His brain is different from other people's. You have no idea. It runs out of him in a stream and it's not always so funny. Gritte can't stay alone with him anymore. She's afraid of him. Come on in, we'll drink some absinthe, and you'll see what I mean."

"This business," says Jaume, "it's a bit like ..."

He doesn't finish his thought. Maybe he has an explanation to give, maybe he wants to see for himself before he makes up his mind.

There's only the little square to cross, and the rain has let up a bit. It takes them no time to get to Gondran's.

Janet is still lying there, stiff and shadowy. Paralysis has turned his scrawny neck into a rigid stake. Under his tawny skin his Adam's apple rises and falls as he swallows tobacco juice. His eyes have fixed, once and for all, on the wall across from the bed, at the spot where they've hung the post office calendar.

Gondran brings out glasses and absinthe. They speak in hushed voices, as though they're staked out for hares.

"He looks bad."

"The tip of his nose is already drooping."

"He won't last much longer."

It almost seems like a form of politeness, when they tell Gondran his father-in-law's going to die soon.

And then, all of a sudden, without warning, *that one* starts up again. At first, he gives a bit of a sigh, like somebody who takes a deep breath before lifting a sledgehammer—nothing to really put the rest of them on guard—but then *wham*! it's on top of them, before they've had any chance to prepare:

"There were little curls of smoke out in the meadow. They were women.

"They were bounding over the bristly grass, with their hair standing straight up like hoopoes' crests.

"They were all different colors—there were bottle-green ones with moon-shaped piercings all sewn up with little red and blue stitches.

"They were *fume*ales, you know—little smoke-ladies. One had an ass like a bale of straw and a chest like a corkscrew, and she was wriggling around so much that her tits were flapping like streamers, going flip, flop, and fuck you too....

"And she was killing fleas by running her tongue under her arms, and scraping herself with lavender till her nails cracked.

"'Strange piece of tail,' I said to myself. I moved ahead, calm and composed as can be. She was so light on her feet it was like they were making music.

"There was another one of them, drinking at the stream, very ladylike. She was scooping up water with an oat casing, stretching her lips back as wide as her hand, baring her lovely teeth, and wiggling her rump in the breeze, like a ripe apple.

"I threw my arms around her. And she pissed on me, the dirty slut..."

"The toad that lived in the willow has come out.

"It has the hands and eyes of a man.

"A man who's been punished.

"It made its home in the willow, out of leaves and mud.

"Its belly is full of caterpillars. But it's still a man.

"It eats caterpillars, but it's a man, you only have to look at its hands.

"It runs its little hands over its belly to check itself out: 'Is it really me,' it's asking itself, 'is it really me?' It has good reason to ask, and then it cries when it's certain it really is him.

"I've seen it crying. Its eyes are like kernels of corn, and the more it cries the more music it croaks through its mouth.

"One day I asked myself: 'Janet, who has any idea what he did to be punished like that, to be left with only his hands and his eyes?'

"These are things that the willow would have told me if I knew how to talk its language. I tried. But there was nothing doing. It was as deaf as a fence post.

"The two of us, the toad and me, once we went all the way to Saint-Michel. It hopped along the bank to watch me.

"I used to say: 'Hey, brother. So, what's new?' When I was watering the meadow it'd follow me around.

"Once, at night, I heard it coming. It was crawling through the mud going *glug, glug* with its mouth to get the worms to come out.

"And so they came along, dancing on their bellies and their backs. One of them was as thick as a blood sausage, all covered in hairs. Another one looked like a diseased finger.

"The toad put its paws on my feet.

"Its little clammy hands on my feet—I hate that. Then it made a habit out of it, the little prancer. Every time it came along I had to be on the lookout, it'd always put its clammy little paws onto my bare feet.

"The time came when I'd had it up to here. The thought hit me just as I was leaving the house.

"The toad was croaking, kind of a low croaking sound. It had a black worm and it was eating it. It had blood on its teeth, and its mouth was full of blood, and it was crying out of its corn-kernel eyes.

"I said to myself: 'Janet, that food's not fit for Christians, you'll be doing a good deed...'

"And I swung my spade at it and lopped it in two.

"It clawed at the ground with its hands. It was chewing at the ground with its bloody teeth. It lay there with its mouth full of dirt, and tears in its corn-kernel eyes..."

When Jaume chances on a wild boar, and his gun is loaded with ten-gauge shot, he hurries to hide himself.

He has something of the same air about him at the moment. Arbaud and Maurras are watching the door.

From outside, Gondran questions them with his eyes. All four of them are scrutinizing each other in silence.

"Well, this is all we needed."

After ten hours of night wind, a brand new day breaks this morning. The first rays of sun pierce through a pristine atmosphere. Having barely taken flight, they're already striking the junipers and thyme on the distant hills. You'd think those parts of earth had moved closer overnight.

"You could really reach out and touch them," Gondran thinks.

The sky is blue from horizon to horizon. The silhouette of the grasses is distinct, and you can make out every shade of green in the patchwork of fields. Here the wind has dropped an olive leaf on a spray of borage; there the lamb's lettuce stands out lighter than the chicory; and here in this corner, where somebody must have shaken out some bags of fertilizer, really dense grasses, almost black, are shooting up like thick hairs on a mole. And you could count the needles at the tops of the pines.

There's something strange too: the silence.

Until yesterday the sky was an arena of sound. Iron-shod mares with carts were rumbling though it at full gallop, whinnying with rage.

Today, silence. The wind has blown beyond all bounds and it's raging on the far side of earth.

No birds.

Silence.

Even the water has stopped murmuring. All the same, if you listen carefully, you can hear its shy, sliding step. Hidden from sight, it's trickling from the pasture to the laneway on its delicate, silvery feet.

Gondran watches the new day break, while he gets his game bag ready. He's going to do some hoeing in his olive grove, in the bottomlands over at Font-de-Garin. It's way down over there behind the three hills that block the valley. To get past them, you have to climb across their navels.

He's carrying his midday meal: a really fresh, firm cheese in its crust of herbs, six cloves of garlic, a vial of oil stopped with a scrap of paper, salt and pepper in an old pill box, a slice of ham, a hefty loaf of bread, wine, a roasted thigh of rabbit rolled up in a vine leaf, and a little pot of jam. All this pell-mell in a leather bag.

In the kitchen Marguerite rakes the coals in the stove with big thrusts of her poker to hurry up the coffee.

The silence outside weighs like lead. Gondran makes the only familiar morning sound as he comes and goes in his hobnailed boots.

Jaume's doves are usually the earliest to stir. The dawn likes to caress them with its supple hands. Today, the dovecote seems dead.

Gondran comes to check the clock and finds out it's only four in the morning.

"Is it working all right?"

"I set it by the sundial just the day before yesterday."

In spite of it all, the silence feels good. The scents of honeysuckle and gorse waft through in big waves. What's more, what good does it do to worry about what earth is getting up to? She does whatever she wants. She's old enough to mind her own business, and she goes about it at her own pace....

"Ain't much sound out there t'day," says Janet.

"You'd think everything had died. Listen...you can't hear anything moving."

"This is bad. Take it from me, boy, it was just like this when it started up the other time..."

"What?"

"...that I can't talk about."

And Janet glues his eyes back to the post office calendar.

Gondran slips his spade through the strap of his leather game bag and hoists it. At the bottom of the stairs he whistles for Labri, his dog, who's asleep under a rose bush. Labri comes out, stretches, yawns, sniffs the bag, and follows. Gondran's reassured to hear the patter of claws behind him.

Past Maurras's meadow—which straddles the slope—the path might as well not even exist. It gradually peters out in the grasses, like a dwindling stream.

This orchard where Gondran's headed—he bought it last year from a guy from Pierrevert who was scraping money together to bid for a postal route.

It's in the Reillanne district, to hell and gone, but he got it for next to nothing, and the olive trees have already paid off. When all is said and done, with next to no effort he gets oil and wood from it. The only thing is, it's far away. And it's that much farther away seeing as there's no road to get there. You have to find your way through hollows, trek along stream beds choked with viburnum and brambles, and then skirt around the hills and take unnamed passes where there are rocks that have the faces of half-formed men.

Gondran's thinking that next time he'd be better off following the hilltops over by Trinquette. The path climbs a bit, but afterward you get a great view the whole way. The air's good and fresh—and you can hear partridges clucking. Over here, the silence is really unnerving. He's thankful for Labri's company.

Seen from the summit of Pymayon, Gondran's orchard looks like a scabby patch in the scrub. All around it, the coat of the *garrigue* is healthy, shaggy, curly. But at this spot, Gondran's spade has scraped it bare.

It's an olive grove that slopes down the fertile side of the hill in an area where the runoff has laid down rich deposits. Below it, the streams have split earth open in a narrow, shadowy cleft, which exhales clammy air, like the mouth of a chasm. A Roman aqueduct straddles it. Its two, spindly haunches, powdery with age, emerge from the olives.

First, Gondran digs a hole under the bushiest juniper in sight. Once he's hit black earth he puts his bottle there to stay cool. He chooses a branch, safe from ants, to hang his bag, and then, with his sleeves rolled up, he sets to work.

His spade's steel rings out amongst the stones.

The shade of the olive trees has shrunk back bit by bit. Just a short time ago it made the whole field look like a carpet patterned with gold. As the sun's rays rose higher, the shadows broke up and grew rounder. Now they're nothing but blue-gray blobs around the bases of the trunks.

It's noon.

The spade stops.

Siesta.

The fly-filled air grates like unripe fruit against a knife. Stretched out flat on the ground, Gondran sleeps heavily.

He wakes all at once. With the same, effortless motion he plunges back into sleep, then comes out of it again. With a start he's on his feet.

Reaching for his spade, he comes face to face with the earth. Why, today, this uneasiness inside of him?

The grasses shiver. The long, muscular body of a startled lizard, cocking its head to the sound of the spade, trembles under the esparto grass.

"Ah, son of a whore!"

The creature advances, bounding like a green stone ricocheting off rocks. It freezes, with its legs bowed; the glowing ember of its gullet puffs and crackles.

In an instant Gondran becomes a tower of strength. Power inflates his arms, bunches up his fists on the grip of his spade, and makes the wooden shaft tremble.

Man wants to be the master-beast, the one who kills. His breath flutters like a thread between his lips.

The lizard comes closer.

A flash, and the spade strikes.

With his boot heel Gondran pounds relentlessly on the writhing stumps.

Now it's nothing more than a clump of quivering mud. Over there, thicker blood reddens the ground. This was the golden-eyed head. The tongue still twitches like a tiny pink leaf, with the unconscious pain of shattered nerves. A paw with little balled-up claws clutches at the dirt.

Gondran gathers himself. There's blood on the blade of his spade. His heavy breathing flows, rhythmic and full. Then his anger dissolves in a deep inhalation of sky-blue air.

Suddenly he's ashamed. With his foot he pushes dirt over the dead lizard.

And there: there it is. The wind comes rushing.

The trees confer in low voices.

The dog's gone. It must have taken off after some wild prey.

Without knowing why, Gondran's ill at ease. He's not sick—he's full of disquiet, and this disquiet sticks in his throat like a stone.

He turns his back on a big tangle of elderberry, honeysuckle, clematis, and figs that moans and writhes more loudly than the surrounding bush.

While he digs, it occurs to him for the first time that there's a kind of blood rising inside bark, just like his own blood; that a fierce will to live makes the tree branches twist and propels these sprays of grasses into the sky.

He thinks about Janet too. Why?

He thinks about Janet and he cocks his eye at the little pile of brown dirt still twitching over the crushed lizard.

Blood, nerves, suffering.

He's caused flesh and blood to suffer, flesh just like his own.

So all around him, on this earth, does every action have to lead to suffering?

Is he directly to blame for the suffering of plants and animals?

Can he not even cut down a tree without committing murder?

It's true, when he cuts down a tree, he does kill.

And when he scythes, he slays.

So that's the way it is—is he killing all the time? Is he living like a gigantic, runaway barrel, leveling everything in his path?

So it is really *all* alive?

Janet has figured this all out ahead of him.

Everything: animals, plants, and who knows, maybe even the stones too.

So, he can't even lift a finger anymore, without unleashing streams of pain?

He straightens himself up. Propped on his spade he surveys the expanse of earth stretching around him, covered with scabs and wounds.

The aqueduct, whose empty channel now funnels nothing but wind, sounds like a mournful flute.

This earth!

Which stretches far and wide, clay-heavy, with her burden of trees and springs, her rivers, her streams, her forests, her mountains and her hills, and her circular towns that whirl amongst shafts of lightning, her hordes of humans clinging onto her coat: what if she really is a living being, what if she really is one body?

With power and bad intentions?

A huge mass that could flatten me, the same way I came down on top of that lizard?

This valley, this fold between the hills, where I scratch away at the soil, what if the whole thing flinched under the sharp edge of my spade?

A body.

And alive.

Life is movement, it's breathing…

It's the voice of the aqueduct and the singing of the trees.

Alive? But absolutely! Because she does move, this earth. Ten years ago she shook hard. Down below, toward Aix, there were whole villages that crumbled, Lambesc, and some others, and the Manosque church bells rang all by themselves, high up in their belfry.

The idea rises in him like a storm.

It wipes out all his reason.

It's overwhelming.

It's hallucinatory.

Along the horizon the rolling hills unwind their snakelike coils.

Earth breathes haltingly.

An immense life force, slow to move, but awesome in its naked power, rouses the stupendous body of earth, flows over her valleys and knolls, folds her flatlands, bends her rivers, and builds up her thick coat of soil and vegetation.

In no time, to avenge herself, she'll haul me up to where the skylarks lose their breath.

Gondran grabs his game bag with one swing of his arm and traverses the hill with long strides, not even daring to whistle for his dog.

He's talked to Jaume about it.

Without any bashfulness.

What's more, ever since, the mystery has turned up everywhere: in the wheat field, under the alfalfa, everywhere. And yesterday, the grove of the three big willows, usually so peaceful, growled at his heels like a guard dog.

This can't go on. It would be best for everybody to talk it through together.

For two evenings they've been mulling it over, huddled around the absinthe bottle.

What matters above all is Jaume's opinion. But Jaume doesn't have much to say. Maurras and Arbaud are there too, their elbows on the table, covering their mouths with their hands.

It's Jaume who knows the hills the best. And on top of that, he reads. Not just the odd newspaper when he goes to town, but books.

Including a copy of *Raspail's Natural Remedies*, and that's serious business.

What matters most is Jaume's opinion.

For the moment, he hardly says anything. He doesn't say "That's impossible." That's what they expect from him. But he doesn't say it. He shakes his head and breathes into his drooping moustache.

"We'll have to wait and see," he decides to say at last.

"So you do think it's possible?"

"We'll have to wait and see."

He suggests that they go down there, tomorrow, with guns.

Agreed.

Who's going?

"Me, I'm going," says Jaume, "and who else?"

The others don't look too sure of themselves.

"Well, for my part," says Maurras, "I'd be glad to go with you, but, honestly, I've got to clean out my stable."

Arbaud stares into his absinthe.

In the end it's decided: Jaume and Gondran will go. The other two will stay with the women.

"After all, we're going to be on our own here too," says Arbaud.

Janet's high-pitched voice threads through the linen curtain and into the kitchen.

"You think I'm raving? Oh, yes, I'm raving. You saw the wind roaring yesterday, didn't you, you smartass? And on the other side of the air? . . . I suppose you'd know, wouldn't you, what's on the other side of the air?"

Young Maurras stops halfway down the steps.

"You'd better make him keep quiet," he says in an undertone, "it's not healthy, that kind of talk."

They've seen nothing.

They've spent the whole day stretched out under the broom grass, hidden by twisted tree branches, with their double-barreled shotguns sticking out from their bodies, like limbs.

But today the clematis is still a clematis, the fig tree still a fig tree. And earth is at rest. Except for a dainty, indecisive squirrel, cocky and abrupt, who crosses the Roman bridge and claws at the sandstone.

The whole day long, without saying a word.

Jaume has chewed on peppermint stems.

When Gondran cleared the saliva that was clinging to his throat, Jaume silenced him with a wave.

Under the grim gaze of their guns the land went on sleeping, verdant, scented.

Step by step, shadow forced the sunlight into retreat.

The evening breeze made the grasses bow over.

Daylight has dropped down on the other side of Lure.

Jaume touches Gondran's arm. They pull back over the stones, flat on their bellies, until they reach cover. With their fluid strides, they make their way back to the Bastides.

Arbaud and Maurras are waiting for them in front of the oak.

"So?"

"Nothing."

But Jaume takes his pipe out of his mouth.

"Let's go to the other side of the tree. There's no need to alarm the women."

Once they're off to the side, Jaume seems to have made up his mind. He talks more than ever:

"To my way of thinking, this is a truly nasty business. When I said to you, 'Let's go,' it was because something happened to me the other morning that really made me wonder. You know, I went to stalk that boar . . . I was on Manin's rise, you know, in the old dovecote. So at daybreak I hear a little pattering overtop of the leaves. 'It's just a young one,' I say to myself. I slide my barrel ever so gently through the slit in the wall and I stay on the lookout. All around, it's dwarf oaks, and there's a little grassy clearing in front. I was staring at the opening where the trail starts. Something that looked like a black ball comes out and it was doing a weird kind of dance. I say to myself: 'That's not it yet, wait a little longer.'

"It jumps again, rolls itself back into a ball. Then it stretches itself out in the sunlight, and then I realize it's a cat.

"A completely black cat.

"So far, so good. It's plopped down on its belly and it's tipping its muzzle up into the shaft of sunlight, then it's lain down on its back and it's combing the grass with its claws, fooling around with the grass blades—all in all, just doing catlike things, the way cats do.

"I kept it in sight. If I didn't fire, it was only because I already knew, or at least I thought I knew...

"And I wasn't wrong. A moment later it lifted itself up on all fours, stiff and straight as a wire, and changed the way it was clowning. It took three steps this way, three steps that, planted itself right in front of that cleft in the hill that lets you see our whole part of the country all the way to Digne. And then it started to caterwaul.... I lifted my barrel and slid it back, ever so gently, not making a sound. I huddled up in the shadow of the dovecote with my hands wrapped around my knees, all hunched up, because that meowing—I recognized it."

All the evening air seems to congeal into silence. Jaume draws twice on his pipe. It's out. He strikes his lighter, gets his pipe going again and, taking a draw, he looks at Gondran, Maurras, and then at Arbaud, who's twirling a straw between his fingers.

"As for the earthquake back in '07," he says after a pause, "it was on a Thursday. The Monday before that, when I was stalking partridge, I'd seen the cat.

"As for the storm on Saint-Pancrace Day, when the flood carried away Magnan's haystack and the baby in its cradle along with the mother who was trying to fish it out, it was on a Tuesday, and on the Sunday before that—I'd seen the cat.

"When the lightning did your dad in, Maurras, in the charcoal makers' hut, I'd seen the cat two days before that.

"Again, I'd seen the cat, I'd heard it meowing, and two days later when I went up into the attic, I found my wife hanging from the skylight.

"When Gondran told us what had happened to him, I knew it had to be this cat. Now listen, I'm telling you all: Stay on the lookout. Every time it shows up, it's two days before earth is going to strike out.

"These hills, you shouldn't trust them. There's sulphur under the stones. You want proof? What about that spring over at Imbert's End, the one that purges your guts every time you swallow a mouthful? It's made of stuff that's foreign to us, but it's alive."

His pipe has gone out again. As usual, he's forgotten to keep drawing through the clay stem. He turns toward Gondran.

"You," he says, "you might be able to get right to the heart of the matter... I mean Janet. I'm not saying this to flatter you, or him. But it is because of him that everything got started.

"It's not to flatter you, or him... you didn't know a thing about it, and neither did he.

"This kind of thing, it always starts with somebody who sees farther than the rest of us. When someone sees farther than the rest of us, it's because there's something a little out of kilter in their brain. Sometimes it could be by nothing at all, just by a hair, but from that moment, it's all over. A horse, it's no longer a horse. A blade of grass, it's no longer a blade of grass. Everything we can't see, they see. Outside the shapes, the outlines we're familiar with, for them there's something extra floating around, like a cloud. You remember what he said about the toad?

"It's like there's somebody next to them explaining everything, laying everything bare.

"We already know a lot about what's happening to us now, and Janet will show us the rest.

"Beyond any doubt, he's bound up in it. He's always been close to earth, more than the rest of us. He used to charm snakes. He knew what all the different kinds of meats taste like—fox, badger, lizard, magpie... He used to make melon soup. He'd take chocolate and grate it into cod stew. Our blood is made from everything we eat, and the brain, it's really nothing but the thickest layer of the blood.

"Listen to him, Gondran, try to learn as much as you can, it will help us out."

The women call them in for supper.

In the gloom, the Bastides are nothing but glimmerings under the trees.

A big star climbs over the hills.

They make their way back.

"Don't shove," Arbaud says quietly to young Maurras, who's hanging on his elbow.

It's morning, two days later. No wind. Nothing but silence. A thick wreath of violets weighs heavily on the unblemished brow of the sky. The sun rises through the mist like a pomegranate.

The air scorches like a sick person's breath.

Young Maurras half opens the door of his stable. He looks at the houses one after the other. They're still sleeping, soundlessly, like tired-out animals. Gondran's place alone is making a soft, rattling sound, behind its hedge.

Maurras goes out, takes two steps into the square, then climbs up on a grain roller to see better. The house has its eyes open—big, watery eyes, which Marguerite's plump shadow passes across like a rolling pupil. The doorway drools a stream of dishwater.

Maurras makes up his mind. He comes up on his noiseless, raffia sandals.

"Gondran," he calls out in a muffled voice that still carries on the morning air.

Gondran appears in the half-opened doorway. He hushes Maurras, with a finger to his lips. Gondran looks like he's still listening a little toward the kitchen, and then he comes out on tiptoe.

"So?" Maurras asks.

"Still the same. A terrible night. My head feels like it's ready to burst. I tried to keep track of things to tell to Jaume, but they're like water—even when you grab them with your fists they run right through. It's like a flock of sheep going by—the noise, the bells, a pair of eyes in every head, a reflection in every eyeball. I saw things in his words...You can't have the slightest idea...It's like having a swarm of bees in my head. I do remember, though—he talked about the cat. Marguerite was drinking coffee. She was making a racket with her spoon, and I shut her up. It was really hard to hear—his voice—it was like oil running out of a broken bottle. He was talking to himself inside, you understand? I cocked my ears as sharp as I could, but that whore of a clock was knocking away, tick, tock, tick, tock. I slid behind the head of the bed. He was saying: "Here kitty, kitty, you in your pretty, pretty coat, you'll freeze your butt out on that bare hilltop. Make yourself a real man's bed. Your claws are like ploughshares, and your tongue's a rasp. It's Janet chatting with you. I'll prune your claws off with a few strokes of my billhook, yes I will."

"He said that, you're sure?"

"For sure. I wrote it down on a bit of newspaper."

"He wouldn't ever have a remedy for all this, ever, would he?"

"A remedy?"

"Yeah, a remedy to sort out this business of the cat. A charm of some kind, I don't know exactly...you know what I'm trying to get at. Some braids of horsehair, a goat's hoof, a parrot's feather, you know, whatever..."

"It's possible, now that you mention it. It is possible. We'd have to go and look at his stash in the willows, you know, where he hides his bottles."

Marguerite opens the door wider and sticks her head out. There are white patches glowing on her cheeks—her peculiar way of going pale. She makes a sign toward her husband:

"Come, come quick."

Maurras is left standing in the morning light, alone.

Now the sky is like a long, blue whetstone that's sharpening the cicadas' scythe. The violet mist begins to invade the lowlands, like a muddy river.

Over the shoulders of the houses you see Arbaud's meadow on the hill, with the mown hay all in windrows, but nobody's thinking of forking it over, or bringing it in; they have other concerns at the moment.

Maurras heads back home. His raffia sandals and the carpet of dust underfoot turn him into a shadow that slides around soundlessly. Even so, when he gets close to Jaume's door, it opens. Alexandre is there in the darkness. All you can see are his mustache and his eyes.

"So?" he asks.

Maurras explains his idea about a remedy.

"That's not where you have to look," says Jaume. "I'm the one who knows, and I'm the one who'll say so, when the time is right."

And then, in an undertone, he adds:

"Above all, we have to keep our eyes on Janet, and there you have it."

He shuts the door, and you can hear him sliding home the bolt.

At Arbaud's house a shutter opens. They're on the lookout there too.

The dreaded day has arrived, slowly but surely, one hour nudging the next along.

They've gone to check out Janet's stash. There are two empty bottles, a bit of chocolate wrapper, and a bizarrely shaped dried root. Maurras has stuck the root in his pocket. Jaume has shrugged his shoulders:

"The remedy has to come from us. These roots, these cypress seeds, all this folderol, it's worth nothing, I'm telling you. The remedy? It's in our arms and in our heads. In our arms most of all. You have to treat these hills rough, like a horse. You know I know their ups and downs like the back of my hand. I haven't hunted all over them for thirty years without getting to know their ways. It's going to jump onto our backs from someplace we're not expecting, and, right away, we'll have to put our best front forward and get our arms moving. Who'll win? We will. There's not even a shadow of a doubt. There'll be a dicey moment or two to get through, but I wager we'll win. It's always been like this. The only thing is, if we're going to win, we can't stand around gaping like a bunch of plaster saints."

Even so, Maurras has put the root in his pocket. Arbaud said, "Let's see it." And he got a look: It resembled a little pitchfork scraped smooth with a knife. He whispered, "Hold on to it, you never know."

At last it was time to fill the women in on what was happening. They were already shocked to see the men neglecting their chores, and all of these hushed conferences around Jaume. "So *that's* what it is," they said. Then each one of them had her own tale to tell. One had seen the cat. Another had heard voices in the trees. Babette mentioned her cupboard muttering away on its own like a fully-grown human being. Marguerite was already in the know. But with her, you'd have to cut your way through three layers of fat to touch any kind of a nerve.

At night, they've barricaded themselves in.

Jaume has carefully loaded all six of the barrels of his three shotguns. His grown-up daughter, as weathered and tanned as a grapevine, weighs the powder in a little scale—"Just a pinch more than we use for wild boar." Then she passes it to her father in the hollow of her palm. It's she who's made sure of the door bolts, stuffed the kitchen drain with a rag, and checked the house out from top to bottom, until her father shouts, "Ulalie, to bed with you."

Babette has prepared a night lamp for the bedroom. Then she's bundled herself up under the sheets with her head against her knees, while her husband gets undressed. When he's ready to get into bed she shows her face: "Aphrodis, did you shut the shed up good and tight? You should have leaned the plough against the door."

And so on and so forth until, in the end, Arbaud has made up his mind to go out. But he hasn't left the room yet before she leaps out of the bed in her nightshirt: "Aphrodis, wait for me, don't leave me alone, I'm going with you!"

Maurras has set up his bed in his mother's room. Their farmhand has come and scratched at the door, in tears. He didn't want to go to bed by himself alone in the attic. They've let him come in and have laid a mattress down on the floor for him.

Gondran and Marguerite have sat down at Janet's bedside, their eyes transfixed, a bitter taste in their mouths, feeling sick with anxiety, mystery, and fear.

And the dreaded day has arrived, slowly but surely, through the course of the night, one hour nudging the next along. And now, look: It's peeking above the hills.

In a single leap the sun clears the crest of the horizon. It enters the sky like a wrestler, atop its undulating arms of fire.

Everybody has rushed outside: the men, the women, the two little girls, Labri the dog. They're in a hurry. They want to get it over with. Since the middle of the night they've been waiting for dawn. Gagou, leaning against his pillar, watches on.

They've gathered under the oak, all of them. Without speaking, they've turned toward Jaume. He's realized that he's in charge. He's conscious of it. It's good this way. He has his two guns strapped across his back. Ulalie follows him, with her own firearm. And it's not just a lady's musket, but a good, stout, double-barreled shotgun loaded on both sides. On her hip, a haversack packed with cartridges.

Babette is there, a little girl on each arm, like a splendid tree ready to march forth bearing its fruits. She's there with her well-scrubbed, lightly powdered girls, in their Sunday best. "You never know…"

Jaume has pulled the men aside.

"Let the women be," he says. "Here's the plan: I'm going up to Les Sablettes. From over there I'll try to figure out what's going on. Maurras, you'll keep a watch over toward Bournes. Gondran, Les Ubacs. Arbaud, Les Adrets. What are we looking for? Everything, and nothing. How moist the air is, how warm, how cold, the wind, the cloud—you can get information out of all of them. So let's go . . ."

He sets off right away, with his long strides. But before he disappears into the thickets of broom grass, he turns around and, cupping his hands, cries out: "It always comes from where you least expect it. Focus on everything, keep your eyes peeled. And, most important of all, if you see the cat, don't shoot."

Then he plunges back into the grass that's up to his shoulders.

The men have left.

And Gagou has come out from between the pillars of his doorway.

He's made his way into the square, over where the women are, with his arms dangling. He's leading with his head, like a dancing marmot.

His lower lip droops, and he's drooling. His chin is shiny with saliva. A grimace—actually a smile—wrinkles his nose and the outlines of his eyes.

Now, in the little square, he lurches heavily and swings his arms. One foot, then the other, one foot, then the other, and then the arms . . . His footsteps go *thwack, thwack*, and dust rises in a rusty, blue plume around him.

Right up till noon they've been keeping watch on all the paths leading to the Bastides.

Nothing has shown up; neither the cat, nor anything else. But who says bad fortune is obliged to travel by road? Isn't there lots of room for it to pass right between the tops of people's heads and the clouds?

Rightly so. Gondran is examining the shapes of the clouds.

There's one weighing down heavily on the hills' back, like a sky-mountain, like a whole country in the sky—a huge, completely deserted country with shaded valleys, sunlight glancing off ridges, terraced escarpments.

Completely deserted...who really knows? There could be celestial mountain people up there, with black beards down to their waists and teeth flashing like suns. It's a whole country above and beyond the country of humans.

Until now Gondran used to study the clouds for the threat of storms, for the white light that warns of leaden hail. Hail is no longer on his mind.

Hail means flattened wheat, hacked-up fruit, ruined hay, and so forth...but what he's on the lookout for now, it's something that threatens him head-on, and not just the grass. Grass, wheat, fruits—too bad for them. His own hide comes first.

He can still hear Janet saying: "So you think you know, do you, you sly devil, what's on the other side of the air?"

And so, Gondran stays absorbed, right until the moment they call out to him from the Bastides.

It was only for lunch.

This peaceful morning has reassured them a little. So has this hearty cabbage and potato soup that sticks to your ribs. It fortifies your blood in an instant and flows fast through your arteries to your brain, full of promise.

"You'll see," says Arbaud, "we'll get away with just a scare."

"We were right to be on guard, for sure, because we'd been warned, but whatever it is, so far it looks like it's just playing around."

They're stretched out under the oak, for siesta.

"Hey you over there, quit that racket!" they yell at Gagou, who's drumming on an empty canister. Then they throw stones at him. And Gagou stops.

It's the silence that wakes them up. A foreign silence. Deeper than usual. More silent than the kind of silence they're used to.

Something has up and left. There's an empty place in the air.

"Hey," says Gondran, alarmed.

Next thing, they're all standing. Something's missing from the background noise of the Bastides. But what?

It's come over them, just like that. Now they're gazing around, craning their necks. They're looking hard at familiar objects: the roller, the harrow, the plough, the winnower. And then back again: the plough, the harrow, the roller . . .

Nothing. Everything's the way it usually is.

But there's something missing.

All of them turn at once toward the fountain.

It's stopped running.

Jaume comes along while they're trying their last resort.

Gondran has wrapped his lips around the spout of the fountain. The iron pipe fills his mouth. He sucks with all his might to get the water to come. With each inhalation, you can hear a gurgling somewhere deep down in the rock. But it subsides just as quickly. The only thing that's fluid is a drop of Gondran's saliva clinging to the iron.

They've all had to give it a try. Now they all have rust on their lips.

"It's too deep," says Jaume. "You won't be able to get to it. But it's true, you weren't around yet when we built this fountain. The pipe runs straight up that bit of a slope, right there, you see? Just about where that little fig tree is. There's a pocket of water up there. If it isn't running, either the pipe is blocked, or else the whole thing's empty from one end to the other. So you can suck all you want, brother. Tomorrow morning we'll have to dig up the pipe."

This morning they've dug up the whole length of iron pipe. It's stretched out on the hill, like a monstrous, pus-covered snake.

That's not where the problem lies.

They've searched for the stone slab over the mouth of the spring. It's under a juniper. They've pried it loose and pulled it up.

Leaning over the hole, they've listened. They can't hear anything flowing.

"Sometimes," says Jaume, "water from springs like this makes no sound. It just oozes out of the ground. But in the end it would fill a whole lake that would last us for life. I'm going down."

He's at the bottom in no time. It wasn't deep. They pass him an oil lamp.

"Hey," Arbaud asks, "how does it look?"

Jaume's voice drifts up with the smoke of the lamp.

"The water's gone. It's completely dry."

"And so," says Marguerite, "how are we going to make his soup and his herb tea?

"I still have a bit in the pail, and I'm going to go fetch what I took down to the goats...."

"What did Jaume say? Didn't he have any idea at all? Doesn't he know if we'll be able to find water anywhere?"

"The rest of us, we'll drink wine, no doubt about that, but your dad?"

"I have barely enough for today, maybe tomorrow, and then what?"

This morning they're hard at work on the hillside before daybreak, all four of them, searching.

They dig until they hit black soil, and then Jaume lowers his face and sniffs.

They dig another hole a little farther on.

Their hopes rise for a moment, when they spot a bunch of rushes. But they're rushes that the old spring had kept alive, and now they're almost dead.

This evening, on the third day, they've come back beat, worn out mostly by disappointment. And they've eagerly knocked back big, cool glasses of wine.

"And so," Marguerite asks again, "how are we going to make his soup and his herb tea?

"I don't have any more.

"Neither does Babeau... Neither does Ma Maurras. Ulalie gave me a pitcher full, just enough for tonight."

Gondran stands under the oak with his whole shaving kit: his razor, his strop, his army mug, his brush, his mirror.

He carries all this pell-mell, squeezed against his chest, except for the mug, which he carries delicately before him between his thumb and his index finger.

In the trunk of the oak there's a nail for his mirror, and the stub of a branch for his towel. All in all, a very convenient setup.

He begins lathering his face. The foam is purple. Jaume looks at him.

"What's that you're shaving with?"

"With wine, of course. I had to do it once before, in Queyras, during maneuvers."

"You're sprucing yourself up?"

"Mainly it's just a good reason to get away from there for a bit," says Gondran, gesturing toward his house.

Jaume pauses for a moment to listen to the razor hissing across Gondran's cheeks. He looks at the fountain. Under the spout the moss is bleached as white as a goat's beard.

"Guess what I'm thinking? Maybe Janet could figure it out for us—where the spring's gone."

"Janet? Hah! Get out of here, he's nothing but a crazy raver."

"Not really as bad as all that. Listen, Médéric, in his day your father-in-law was famous for knowing a lot about water. Well-diggers used to come around to ask him questions before they started digging. When he was still down on the plain, I remember a Monsieur Boisse—who was building fountains in those days—came looking for him in a car, for that very reason. That was before you married Marguerite. Janet's the one who found our pocket of water. 'Dig here,' he said, 'it isn't deep, I can feel it.' At first we laughed all around, but then we felt obliged to try digging where he said, and sure enough, we found it. I want to go see him."

"If you want."

Gondran scrapes away at his chin with delicate care. There's a little dimple right at the tip, where he always cuts himself.

"So, Papa Janet, how's it been going since the last time I saw you?"

"He doesn't recognize you," whispers Marguerite.

Janet takes clear aim at his daughter with his gaze.

"She's nuts, that one. Not recognize you? So what, you think I've flipped, too?"

"Hey, his hearing's still good..."

Jaume sits down at the foot of the bed, directly in line with Janet's stretched-out body—now nothing but skin and bones, looks, and words.

"How's it going, Janet?"

"Bad. And it's not about to go any other way."

"Are you in pain?"

"In my head."

"You have a headache?"

"No. It's not aching like other people's. It's full...just full, and it's cracking up all by itself, in the dark, like an old washbasin. They leave me on my own all the time. I can't talk to anybody, so it builds up inside me, it weighs on my bones. A bit of it runs out through my eyes, but the big pieces, they can't make it through, so they stay inside my head."

"Big pieces of what?"

"Of life, Jaume."

"Pieces of life? What do you mean?"

"Oh, you'll find out....

"I remember everything I've done in my life. It comes to me in big blocks, piled up like rocks, and it pushes out through my flesh.

"I remember everything.

"I remember that I picked up a piece of string on the Montfuron road when I was going to the fair at Reillanne. I fixed my whip with it. I see the string, I see the whip, I see the cartwheel, just like I saw it when I bent down to pick up the string. I see the hoofs of the mule I owned at the time.

"On the wall over there, I see all of that, all the time: the string, the whip, the wheel. When I close my eyes, it stays there in my head.

"It's like that with everything I've done.

"Now that I've told you about it, it's gone down a little."

"You remember everything?"

"Everything. Even things—"

"Things?"

"I mean things that you do sometimes, thinking they'll go away, but they stick around anyway. And then, down the road, you run into them again, head on. They're waiting for you."

"Bad things?"

"What, you think you can tell what's bad from what's good?"

Jaume falls speechless. In the old man's talk there are chasms where untold powers rumble.

"Gritte, some water."

He's put on a different voice to demand a drink.

Marguerite comes obligingly with a tiny bit of water in a cup.

"Do you have any more?" Jaume asks in an undertone.

"This is some holy water I'd put aside for Palm Sunday. It was in the armoire. It's just as well that it gets used for something."

"Janet, since you remember everything, shouldn't you be able to remember the day when you found the spring?"

"Yes. You were one of those who laughed. You too."

"Who could've possibly guessed that there'd be water there?"

"You're all the same. You always want to understand: This one does this…why? This one does that…why? Let the people who really know what they're doing get on with it. Did I find it? Yes or no?"

"You found it."

"And was it good water?"

"It was good water."

"What more do you want?"

In an instant Jaume makes up his mind.

"I'd like to know how you did it. How you have to root around in the ground, or if there's some kind of a plant that shows you where there's water running underneath."

"Have a look and see if you can find my wad."

"Where?"

"There, under the sheet, take a little peek."

Jaume finds the wad of tobacco, already chewed up, still moist.

"Give it to me."

Janet slips it into his mouth.

"Do you know the song, Alex?"

At Pertuis fair
If you don't pay
The stable boy
Will snatch your hay.

Janet beams. Tobacco juice trickles from the corner of his mouth.

"Ah, you old rascal," says Jaume good-naturedly, "you're being cagey. Don't you want to tell me your secret for finding water?"

"My boy, it just isn't possible. Either you're born with it or not, and if you're not, nothing doing! It's your mother's womb that transmits it. You have to get going on it way ahead of time. Now it's too late.

"What, the water you have already isn't good enough? You're saying my water isn't any good? Water that comes right out of our own hill, water you'll never find the equal of."

Jaume's going to tell him that the spring has failed, but Marguerite is already shushing him with her stubby finger.

Anyway, now it's clear beyond a doubt: Janet won't say a thing, whether out of deceitfulness, sickness, or spite.

"I knew it," Gondran says, coming back in. "What can you make of that?" He points toward Janet, who has finally fallen silent. "He's all bad, rotten from head to toe."

The hardest time is from noon onwards.

For the past two days it seems as though the sun has leapt closer to earth. Its molten mass is crackling right at the edge of the sky. Heat descends from it like a heavy downpour. Wide, rippling whirlwinds blur the air.

There's nothing to drink but wine, and your parched throat craves it constantly.

Thirst is ever-present.

They fill their hours with expansive dreams of dancing, silver waters.

Everything's ready for the expedition: ropes, canteens, the gas lighter, the alpenstocks, the shotgun. Now they only have to wait for night to fall. It won't be long now—the sky's already green, and banks of cloud, pinkish just a moment ago, are gradually turning blue. What's left of the blinding dust of the sun is settling into a bowl on the horizon. Lure's shadow is rising.

Here's what they're going to do: Since they've found out from Maurras that he's seen Gagou twice coming back at dawn with his pants all muddy and his hair dripping wet, tonight they're going to follow him. He has to have found a spring. So they'll find out for sure.

It goes without saying that they'd prefer not to be heading out into the wasteland during the night, but it's the only way.

And after all, there's the moon. Look: The shadow of the cypress is already growing darker by the minute and taking shape on top of the grass.

With raised voices, they bid each other good evening. They walk across the square. Doors slam and, even more loudly than usual, shutters bang. They've got to make Gagou believe they're going to bed.

A light, evening breeze stirs in the foliage of the oak. A nightingale sings.

"There he is," Jaume whispers.

The moon plainly lights up the two mossy pillars and the sheet-metal shack. Gagou comes out. He's wearing only his britches. His upper body is naked, and his oversized head tilts toward the moon. In the whitish light he stretches back his drooling lips. A varied kind of clucking issues from his mouth. He's singing.

He's dancing too. The moonlight infuses him with mild agitation. He moves about lightly, as though he were gliding over the tips of the grass blades without even moving his feet. His hips sway. He totters, drunk with the dusk. He comes out from between the pillars.

In a flash he takes off, as though he were launching himself into the night.

"Let's let him get ahead a bit," says Maurras, "he has a keen ear. This is definitely the way he comes back in the morning. I know he goes past La Thomassine. We won't lose him."

After you leave the clump of trees around the Bastides it's just an empty plain on both sides of the path that Gagou's following. It's as naked as your hand and it rises gently toward the high ridge of Mount Lure.

You can see him up ahead walking the whole way as though he were dancing.

"Let's go."

Jaume gets up, and so does Maurras. Arbaud and Gondran are going to keep watch over the women.

"I would have been much happier to wait for Ulalie," says Jaume. "She took off again this afternoon, and she's been coming back late. She's been out looking for water, too. Gondran, keep an eye on her, and tell her to sleep at your place. That way she won't be alone."

After you've gone past La Thomassine there are two roads. Two "roads"—that's generous. Let's say that, from there, you can head off in one of two general directions. On one side you drop down gradually until you reach a dry creek bed. You follow it and you come out at Plaines on the road to Reillanne. On the other side it's nothing but another empty plain, but one that rises slightly. You pass through a cleft in the rock and you get to a big, hollowed-out bowl, directly below Mount Lure. Nothing but desert. In the middle of the valley you find the dusty remains of an uninhabited village. There are five of them like this below Lure. This one they abandoned because of the 1883 cholera. There were a hundred deaths here, ten in one day. There were only about twenty women and children left, who fled the mountain with bundles over their shoulders. At night, through the fields, they slipped into the towns on the plain below. Since then, not a soul. The houses are half fallen down. In the streets filled with nettles the wind rages, chants, bellows, howls its music through the cavities of the shutterless windows and out through the gaping doorways.

Gagou heads off in the direction of this village.

"Hey," says Maurras softly.

They stop. Gagou's footsteps ring out clearly ahead of them.

"He's going up top."

"So it seems."

"Do you feel good about going there at night?"

"Together, yes. Alone, I'd be heading back. But there's two of us. More than that, we have got to know where he's getting his water."

The moon turns Gagou into an unearthly being. Instinctively, now that he's out in the wild, he's taken on the restless, slicked-back look of an animal. His spine is arched, his neck is drawn down into his shoulders. He advances with his head tilted forward. His lanky arms dangle almost to the ground, like paws. He's doubled in this posture by a monstrous, quadruped shadow, which leaps forward by his side.

He keeps on changing his song-like cry. At times his gait again takes on the air of a dance, and then his voice scatters farther afield, sharper and more ecstatic.

When they're about to pass through the notch in the rocks, Maurras whispers "Hey!" one more time, and stops Jaume.

"Listen."

"Yeah, just a moment ago, I did too."

"On the left?"

"On the left."

"That's weird. That's over by Imbert's End. Who could that be?"

"No idea."

They can hear what sound like footsteps on the slope of the hill, as though somebody was walking beside them along a parallel path.

Some stones roll down the slope. Gagou keeps moving up ahead.

They go back to walking gingerly, with their ears cocked.

"It's somebody who knows the way."

"Can't you see anything, you with your sharp eyes?"

Maurras can't see a thing, but he stays put and holds Jaume back by the arm.

"Jaume, let's go back. Listen to me. Other than the two of us and Gagou, who could be out at night, walking toward this village, in this wasteland? Who? Unless . . .

"You know as well as anybody. It's no fairy tale—since the cholera, things happen up here that it's better not to stick your nose into. You saw that shepherd from Les Campas when they carried him back down on some fence-posts. You saw him? He didn't die an easy death. Did you see his eyes? And his neck twisted up like a well-rope."

For a moment, Jaume is taken back there, not saying a word. Maurras's voice lingers, living on inside of Jaume's head. He did see the dead shepherd, did see the twenty dead sheep, the dead dog, the clouds of flies swarming through the deserted street.

He bleats out, in a muffled voice:

"I know, César, but what about the water?"

He's spoken the word that needed to be said, for Maurras, and for himself. It's water—the memory of water—that pushes them on. The night air brushes their cheeks like a refreshing promise. In front of them, the body of Lure looms up, massive: the mother of waters, the mountain that stores water in the dark recesses of her porous body. Somewhere in the distance, the flute-like song of a spring is quavering. From amongst the grasses a big, flat rock shimmers like a watery eye. Moonlight pours down from the top of the heavens and sprays back upwards as a white mist. Gagou's shadow swims through it like a fish.

"You didn't hear anything more?"

"No. Maybe it was somebody from Villemus on his way home."

"We'd better hope so."

"It's not far from there to the Eyries road. Maybe it was somebody from up top coming back by the shortcut. Yesterday was fair day in Manosque."

"Once in a while there's a fancy-ribbon man out on the road."

"Once in a while."

And right there, across their path, lies the skeleton of the village. It's nothing more now than a pile of broken bones lashed by the wind. The long, drawn-out current of the air howls through the vacant houses. Fragments of bone gleam beneath the moonlight.

In the wind's hollow the village lies motionless. Grasses swell around it like the sea.

Gagou follows a well-worn path through the nettles. Now he's fluttering and leaping like a dead leaf, as though the wind were toying with him.

Maurras and Jaume straddle the fallen beams and stones with care. But they still can't stop the canteens slung over their shoulders from clattering.

"This is the worst time to make any noise, laddy," says Jaume, who's halted flat on his stomach, on top of a mound of rubble. "I think we've found it. Let's leave all the tins under the brambles. We'll come back for them in a minute."

The houses cast a shadow, shaped like a saw, onto the street. From time to time it seems as if a window is lit up from within, but no, it's only one that's open more directly to the moonlight. This same cold light inhabits hearths long since bereft of crickets. It sharply defines shadows shaped like hooded men, who keep vigil in rooms with sunken floors, amid the riot of nettles and hawthorns.

There's a barn, almost intact, with an arch-topped door, and a bit of straw sticking out. It's through here that the shepherd of Les Campas disappeared that evening, in a heavy downpour, along with his flock and his dog—the whole lot of them, just as they were hurrying by on this side.

Gagou takes a single leap and vanishes.

Jaume lifts his nose, takes a long sniff.

"I smell water."

As they arrive at the top of the climbing street, suddenly they see: It's a square.

The facades of the houses are still standing upright. A lopsided balcony supports a broken flagpole and a placard where you can still read "Republican Club." Grass is growing in between the paving stones. A mulberry tree makes cooing sounds as it's tousled by the moon's wan hand.

In the middle of the square a venerable fountain thrusts out the belly of its basin. Aside from Mount Lure and the trees, this must be the most ancient thing in the whole district. Harness bits have rubbed and worn away its rim. A pillar with bronze spouts rears up above the circular basin. Four marble-cheeked cherubs are blowing with their mouths around the pipes . . . and there's no water coming out. Even so, the basin is brimming with clear liquid. In its abundance it streams over the paving stones, and its force has undermined them. Huge horsetails have sprung up through the pavement. This pillar, it's alive, like somebody shivering inside a coat. Spring water oozes from the moss up and down its whole length. There's nothing dry except the four cherubs' heads, whose marble masks gaze at the lifeless houses.

Gagou is there, sprawled over the water. His arms are churning away like a millwheel, and water is gushing up around him. It's getting all over him—his hair, the down on his chest, his scrawny back. And you can hear it sluicing down the legs of his canvas pants.

Now he's drinking.

With outstretched arms he grabs hold of the basin, this gigantic, overflowing goblet, and presses his mouth against a crack in the rim. Between mouthfuls he moans with pleasure like a nursing infant.

The two men observe this manic glee. Their own joy is more restrained. It ripens inside their minds like a giant sunflower.

"We'll have to clean out the basin," breathes Jaume.

"And fix the pipe," says Maurras.

"We'll come with the canteens and take turns," says Jaume.

"Take turns, just like in the army," says Maurras.

There they are, in the shadows, twin statues in the recess of a shrine. As they breathe words back and forth, the bloom of their joy spreads out wider than the sun's rays.

"I'm going for the canteens," says Jaume.

"And, all things considered," says Maurras, drawing his absinthe toward him, "it's just as well that Jaume didn't see what I saw."

He drinks. Gondran takes the opportunity to drink too; he wouldn't have wanted to break the thread of the story.

"There and back—to the fountain and back to the brambles—takes almost a quarter of an hour. By then, the moon was shining full on the square. It was just like daylight. Between where the club used to be and the old bakery, there's a little laneway, short and straight. The moon had filled it with light. You'd have said it was a bar of pure silver. Jaume had just left, and at the far end of the lane I saw a black shape coming toward me, tall, thin, so thin that at first I thought I was dreaming. Then it got bigger and, just like that, it was right in front of me, ten yards the other side of the fountain. I stayed still for a moment, you know, 'cause I was pounding away pretty hard under my shirt.

"This skinny thing was looking at Gagou. Little by little, I got to saying to myself: 'But, César, that's not Ulalie, is it?' It sure seemed like it was her, anyways.

"And go fuck yourself if she doesn't whistle, and my boy Gagou lifts up his nose. Right then and there, as though it was all set up in advance. He lifts his head, he sees her, he runs toward her. They must be used to it. It was as regular as clockwork.

"She leans her gun against the wall..."

Maurras goes silent. He looks mistrustfully around him. He's alone with Gondran for sure, in the kitchen where Janet is sleeping with his eyes wide open. Janet doesn't matter, but the door to the bedroom is ajar, and you can hear Marguerite beating out a mattress.

He winks: "Go shut the door." Gondran comes back and sits down.

"So, she leans her gun against the wall. She lies down, hauls up her skirt, spreads her legs, and there you have it—my man Gagou's on top of her."

"That!" says Gondran, dumbfounded. He strikes the table with his fist. "That, now... no."

"It was just the way I'm telling you. I got a good look from where I was. Gagou was lying on top of her. They knew the drill. And this business must have been going on for a while."

"That, now," says Gondran, "that, you know..."

As he watches him wrestle awkwardly with the overwhelming news, Maurras savours Gondran's astonishment.

"Between you and me," Maurras goes on, "Jaume's daughter—she may be stupid, worn-out, whatever you want to call her, but when you come right down to it, she has the skin of a woman, like any other. To do it with her you'd have to have served in the Foreign Legion. She found somebody who'd have her..."

"I'm not saying that," grumbles Gondran, "I'm not saying that. But to do it with Gagou... Somebody must have diddled that girl. And, so, what did you do?"

"I watched them kick their legs up in the air for a minute or two, then I thought it would be better to make them leave before Jaume got back, so I fired a shot into the air.

"I told him I'd fired to make Gagou take off. But between you and me, Médéric, eh, between you and me, for goodness' sake, it's not really worth his putting on such airs and graces about her."

It was Gondran who made the first trip to the ghost village to fetch water for everyone. He went in broad daylight, with the cart and the mule. He brought back five big earthenware jars full.

Now Jaume has drawn up a list of names: ARBAUD, GONDRAN, JAUME, MAURRAS, in alphabetical order. He's nailed it to the trunk of the oak. That way, there's no argument. When your turn comes up, you go.

Even so, it's Gondran who's ended up going first, because today

Arbaud can't even think about water. His little girl is sick—Marie, the older one.

For two days she's been shivering, in spite of the sultry, stagnant air. She must have swallowed a bellyful from the cistern that's only safe for the animals. It came over her just the other evening, and her cheeks are already hollow. It doesn't matter how often she runs her tongue over her cracked lips to soften them, the fever keeps hardening them again. There are big dark rings circling her sparkling eyes.

This morning she's started to perspire. They've had to change the sheets on her bed—she was completely sticky with sweat.

Babette has to be there next to the bed, to cry over and over: "My little one, my little one, my little one," as though she's trying to force blind fate to understand what an injustice it is to make her little one suffer.

Arbaud has gone to find Jaume, who's come with his book, a *Raspail* covered with wrapping paper.

This book had won its reputation on the strength of Jaume being heard to say: "I bought it the year I got married, after I'd been wanting it for three years."

He flips through the pages and runs down the index with his finger:

"That's it, you see."

He thrusts the page where it's listed under Arbaud's nose.

"That's it, definitely, you see . . ."

They read together, spelling out the words. From time to time Jaume lifts his head and stares at the ceiling, like a person who's struggling to make sense of something.

"So, what is it?" asks Arbaud. "Is it serious?"

"No, you can see, it's written right here. A doctor would stick you with fifteen francs worth of drugs, and then order you to fast—what more could you possibly want? Now this, this here is the poor people's doctor, and a tough one too, take my word for it. Let's see what he says: 'Tisane of borage . . .' Do you have any borage?"

"Yes, yes," says Babette.

"...'toast a slice of bread, soak in sweet wine and apply it to the soles of the patient's feet'... that's not hard to do!...'Scutcheon: a cotton compress sprinkled with eau de vie and impregnated with incense smoke...Also apply a scutcheon to the patient.' Here, I'm marking everything down for you on this piece of paper. If you can't remember it properly, come back and see me, I have the book."

"So you're sure it's nothing then?" asks Babette, accompanying Jaume to the doorway. "Are you sure?"

"Don't worry, I'm certain of it, it's all written down right here."

He taps the book with the flat of his hand, to vouch for it.

"We have *got*," says Babette coming back in, "to buy one of those books."

Notwithstanding the scutcheon and the borage tisanes, Marie is still sick. Her tiny hands look like porcelain. She gazes out from deep within herself.

Through her skin you can see the fire that's consuming her, licking at her bones. She's flat out, thin as a crucifix. She can't even lift a hand to chase away the flies, and lets them wander over her face. When they come close to one of her eyes, she moves her lids a little.

Red-eyed, Babette battles alongside her daughter. She's overturned all the boxes of medicinal plants—the dried herbs folded in newspaper: camomile, mallow, sage, thyme, hyssop, agrimony, aspic, artemisia...

She's opened all the packets and spread them across the table. Her daughter's well-being is bound up in these flowers. Water is already bubbling in the saucepan over the fire. All it will take is to throw the right herb in, and tomorrow Marie will feel better. As Babette shuffles through them on the table, the paper packets sound like ripe wheat shaken by the wind.

Jaume is afraid.

Ever since the morning when he found himself in charge, he's been battling, sustained by hope. He's been like a coiled spring: he absorbs a blow, and it propels him forward. Now, this evening, he's plunged headlong into a torrent of despair, and the raging waters are carrying him away.

He's afraid. He's no longer sure they're going to win in this battle against the hills' ill will. Doubt is bristling inside him like a thistle.

It started with Maurras.

A short time ago Jaume had said to him:

"César, tomorrow you'll be going for water."

And César shot back: "No!" It was the first time anybody had refused an order.

"I'll go when I want to, when *I* want to, you hear? You have no right to order me around. Do I owe you something? Because, if I do owe you something, just say so, and I'll pay you. And if I don't owe you anything, then leave me alone for fuck's sake, you with your orders. We aren't children, we know what we need to do—"

"But César, we had an agreement."

"We didn't have any kind of agreement. It was you who wrote up the list on your own. And who gave you the right, in the first place? Who are you around here, the pope?"

"Good, that's fine, I'll go myself," Jaume said, "I'll go in your place."

And Maurras, as he was heading off, turned around to reply:

"Send Ulalie. She knows the way."

It can't go on like this. With somebody in charge there was still a chance—when the one in the lead knew how to...

A doubt grips his heart: Does he really know?

"Do I have what it takes to wrestle the rage of these hills? I'm full of good intentions...and that's all. I got everybody to stand on guard, but bad luck snuck in amongst them anyways. It flew right over our heads and picked out what it wanted, without a care, like it was at home: the fountain, Marie...

"It's always there. I feel like I can hear its giant wings moving at night. It's lying in wait...

"Who's next?"

All night long he lay sprawled out on top of his hopes and fears. By morning he had only one thought: to go and see Janet. Janet must know the key to all of this.

And daylight broke.

Marguerite, dazed with having to dance around the sick bed day and night, is stumbling around on inflamed feet. When Jaume comes in, she's fallen asleep standing up in front of her open sideboard, with no idea what she's come looking for.

"Gritte, go and lie down if you want to," says Jaume, "make the most of my being here. I'm going to spend a little time with your father."

No sooner were they alone, than Janet spoke up first, as though he'd seen in advance, through the walls, that Jaume would be coming.

"You'll be staying till dark if you want to say everything."

"Janet, there's nothing to make fun about this time. Listen to me. I hadn't found the guts to talk to you yet, but now I have to. Listen to me: If you want to save us, you can. I've seen the cat."

Janet is dead wood. He can't even shiver anymore. Suddenly he's shut his eyelids.

He reopens them. His gaze shoots toward Jaume.

"Shift my head for me, I can't see you properly, and for what we have to talk about we have to be able to see each other."

Jaume takes hold of Janet's head and gingerly turns it toward himself.

"That's better. So you saw it. When?"

"Three weeks ago."

"And it's only now you've come to tell me?"

"I thought I was strong enough to stand up to it, like they say you stood up to it once, but I'm afraid at this point things aren't going so well."

"You've counted the hills' teeth?"

"Their teeth?"

"You've looked to see if their coat is standing up straight, or laying down a little in the direction of the wind?"

"..."

"You've spoken in tongues with the crow's wife?"

"..."

"You've squinted?"

"..."

"You've been to see the cat-witch's nest on the other side of Espel Hill, where there's nothing but broom-grass that the cat scorches with her own breath?"

Jaume asks himself if this is the same man, so bitter and clipped just a minute ago, who's talking this way.

It is the same man: the same look, the same mouth stained with tobacco juice.

"No, I haven't done any of those things."

"So what *have* you done, then?"

"Me, Janet? I've said to them: 'Keep your eyes on all the paths, in case anything wild, with bad intentions, happens to come along…'"

"So, while we were keeping our eyes peeled, something messed with the fountain, and it failed. I searched for the water, I rooted around in the ground, then I racked my brains. In the end we found water in that village way up there, you know where I mean? Now Arbaud's daughter has taken sick. Something completely unheard of that even my book doesn't know about, and she's getting thinner and thinner, to the point where she's as small as a bird. She can barely open her mouth to say 'mama.' It's pathetic.

"The most frightening thing is that it's gotten inside people's heads. Maurras's already... Inside people's heads where nobody can see a thing, where evil goes about its business, quietly, not revealing itself, not showing any sign, not even making a bump... ever so smoothly, ever so smoothly.

"As long as we're united, we can win. It's hard to break through a bundle of sticks. But if it's every man for himself, groping around blindly, nobody knowing anything, we'll all be done for, one after another.

"I'm afraid for the Bastides."

"Jackass."

"..."

"You're a jackass, I tell you. And he wants to be the leader, does he... Ah, so you've seen the cat; good. And you've posted the men out on all the paths?"

He laughs—his mouth splits open like a block of wood.

"And you'd rather I didn't call you a jackass?"

His voice is getting deeper and huskier. He's made of stone. His eyes aren't blinking. He's like a hollow, windblown stone.

"You're fucked."

"Don't say that, Janet. It sounds like you're glad about it."

"I am glad. There are always way too many jackasses like you."

"Why are you talking like this? Do you have a problem with somebody?"

"With all of you."

"What have we done to you?"

"You're always right there in my face, with your legs marching back and forth, your arms swinging around like branches, your bellies stretched tight. You've haven't even thought of giving me a little bit of your life. Just a little bit. I'm not asking for much of it, just enough for me to fill my pipe and go and sit down under the tree."

"You know very well, Janet, that it's impossible. You shouldn't hold it against us. And on top of that, don't you care at all about the Bastides? This bit of earth that's ours, these houses where we've all been through so much—good times and bad. What about Marguerite? What about Gondran, who makes absinthe for you just the way you like it?"

" 'e doesn't give me anymore since I've been sick."

"And Arbaud's little girls, who have barely started out in life, and Babette, who came up here from Pertuis to live with us and never had a second thought. None of them are ready to give it up for good."

"I'm good and ready, I am."

"And your fields—those clearings in amongst the trees, your olives, your delicious cantaloupes. Don't you think about all these things, even a little? Would you like it all to go back to being grassland? "

"All of it. It's a pain in the arse for me. I'm moving forward; all that's behind. Where I'm going, I won't have any need of it."

"You're selfish."

"I don't give a fuck.

"And I'm saying to you one more time: it's over. You don't even have a month left. And you know, when I say something, it's true.

"Remember your wife? Hadn't I warned you. True, or not? You found her hanging, didn't you? And your daughter, getting herself banged by that slobberer..."

Jaume started. The chair toppled behind him. He grabbed Janet by the neck.

"You," he said, and the words sprayed out between his clenched teeth, "I've had enough of your vicious tricks. You're worse than a wolf. You know you haven't a right to say a word about my wife, you of all people. Or about my daughter... If you were in your right mind I'd smash your face in. So, don't go on asking for it."

Jaume gathers himself, gulps some air, turns his ear toward the bedroom where Marguerite is sleeping.

He stands his chair back up and sits down. He's regained control of himself.

Janet looks dead, but you can hear his chuckles nibbling away at the silence.

"Janet, I didn't come here to argue. You see, I'm calm now. It's not just me who could suffer, it's everybody. Think about it. If you know what we need to do, say it."

"I'm about to tell you...It's a bit complicated. You have to see things from above, like you were at the top of a tree, as though the whole of earth were spread out underneath you."

Janet is panting—the rapid panting of a bird. He's closed his eyes. He's looking inside himself, at the cellar in his chest where so many things have piled up over eighty years.

And all of a sudden it comes unblocked. It flows—thin, thick, thin again, lees and wine mixing together, as if a neglected barrel had popped its bung.

"You want to know what you need to do, only you don't even know what kind of world you're living in. You realize something's against you, but you don't know what. And all this because you've been staring at what's around you without really seeing it. I bet you've never given any thought to the great power?

"The great power of animals, plants, and rock.

"Earth isn't made for you alone to keep on using the way you've been used to, on and on, without getting some advice from the master every once in a while. You're like a tenant farmer—and then there's the landlord. The landlord in his handsome, six-button jacket, his brown corduroy vest, his sheepskin coat. Do you know him, the landlord?

"You've never heard him hissing like the wind across a leaf, a leaf-let just unfolding, a newborn leaf on a dappled apple tree. It's his loving voice. He talks that way to animals and trees. He's the father of everything. He has the blood of all things in his veins. When rabbits run out of breath, he lifts them up in his hands:

"'Ah, my lovely one,' he'll say, 'you're soaking wet, your eyes are rolling around in your head, your ears are bleeding, have you been running for your life? Settle down here, between my legs. Don't be afraid, you're safe now.'

"The bittersweet sanctuary, and the stream of...

"Then it's the dogs who race up.

"When you say to yourself: 'My dog's gone off hunting on his own,' it's because he's shaken you off to go see the landlord.

"The handsome, six-buttoned jacket, and the bowl of the bell on the neck of the sheep.

"And in the shelter, between his legs, the dog and the rabbit get friendly, nose to nose, coat to coat. The rabbit sniffs your dog in the ear, your dog shakes its ear because the rabbit has breathed into it. He looks around and he has the air of saying: 'It's not my fault if I've chased it all day through broom-grass, and up and down furrows, and the pools in the stream. There are weeds in there, like twine, that bind your hands and feet.'

"That's when everybody turns up: the turtledove, the fox, the snake, the lizard, the mouse, the grasshopper, the rat, the weasel, and the spider, the moorhen, the magpie, everything that walks, everything that runs. There are roads full, you might even go so far as to say streams full of animals. It's a stream that's singing and leaping and it flows and rubs at the sides of the path and tears away lumps of earth and carries away whole limbs from hawthorns the stream has uprooted.

"And they all come because he's the father of caresses. He has a word for each one of them:

"'Tourturtle, take route, tooraloo; fox, phlox, flame-in-a-box.'

"He teases tufts of fur toward himself.

"'Lachrymizard, muse, musette, calf's muzzle wedged in a bucket.'

"Next he's going to take a stroll through the trees.

"For the trees, it's the same. They know him. They're not afraid.

"You—you've never known anything but trees that are on their guard. You don't know what a tree really is. Around him, they behave the same as they did during the first days of the world, before we'd cut a single branch.

"...There were woods, and no sound of the axe yet, or of the pruning hook. No knife blade yet on the hillside. The woods on the hillside, and no axe.

"He passes alongside, in his sheepskin jacket. Linden trees make sounds like weeping cats, the chestnuts sound like women moaning, and the plane tree creaks from inside itself, like a man begging for charity.

"He sees their wounds—the knife stabs and the clefts from the axe—and he soothes them.

"He speaks to the linden, the plane tree, the laurel, the olive, the olive grove, the savory, and the newly planted vine, and it's for all this—the pomegranate too—it's because of his compassion that he's master, and that they love him and obey him.

"And if he wanted to wipe the Bastides right off this tiny bump of a hill, 'cause humanity has done too much harm, it's no big deal for him. Just like it's no big deal to let himself be seen by jackasses. He just puffs a little breeze into the daylight, and it's done.

"He holds the great power in his hand."

"Animals, plants, rock!

"It's strong—a tree. A hundred years it's spent holding up the weight of the sky, with a hopelessly twisted branch.

"It's strong—an animal. Especially the little ones.

"They sleep curled up in the grass, all on their own in the wide open world.

"All alone curled up in the grass, and the whole world circling 'round.

"They have stout hearts. They don't cry out when you kill them. They fix your eyes and then they pierce them with their own, like needles.

"You haven't spent enough time watching animals die.

"It's strong—a rock, one of those big rocks that part the wind in two. Standing for who knows how long? A thousand years?

"One of those rocks that have been in the world forever—long before you, Jaume, before the apple and olive groves, before me, before the woods and the rest of the animals. Before the fathers of all this—of you, me, the apple. Before the time, Jaume, when the father of all of this might have been nothing but a swelling in his own father's loincloth.

"One of those rocks that was around on the first day and have always been the same, never changing, for who knows how long? That's what you have to know to get at the remedy."

Jaume listens. He feels the world rocking under his feet, like the floorboards of a rowboat.

His head is full of images of earth: He sees trees, plants, animals —from the grasshopper, to the wild boar—and for him it's all part of this truly solid world, where he moves along familiar grooves.

And now?

There's no way he would have believed that Janet could be so strong. To begin with, it's this glimpse of power that's frightened him. This time, somebody *in the know* is talking.

And *him*, he really does know. Everything that was obscure till now is becoming clear. Incomprehensible things are being explained. But what's coming to light in this way is terrifying.

The old ways were so straightforward. There was humanity, and all around, but underneath, animals and plants. And things were going along well that way. You kill a hare, you harvest a fruit. A peach—it's nothing but sweet juice in your mouth; a hare—it's a heaped-up plateful of rich, dark meat. And afterward, you lick your lips, and you smoke a pipe on the front step.

It was simple, but it left a lot of things in the dark.

From now on it's going to be necessary to live in a lit-up world, and it's painful.

It's painful because it's not just humanity anymore, with everything else underneath, but there's a giant ill will and, way down below, humanity tossed in together with the animals and the plants.

He can feel the hill—alive and terrible—moving under his feet.

"Now, I'm going to tell you the secret."

Jaume would be happier if Janet kept quiet for the moment.

"I'm going to tell you. Everything's sickly sweet, like a corpse.

"There's too much blood around us.

"There are ten holes, there are hundreds of holes in the flesh of living creatures and in living wood, and out of them the blood and the sap flow over the world like a gigantic river, like the Durance.

"There are a hundred holes, there are a thousand holes we've made with our hands.

"And the master no longer has enough saliva and soothing talk to heal them.

"When all is said and done, these animals, these trees, they're his, they belong to him—to the landlord. His sheepskin jacket—it's the sheep who gave it to him, without having to skin itself, without bleeding, just so; and the sheep-bone buttons, just so, without bleeding; the button-bones, the sheep...

"You and I, we belong to him too. Except that for some time now we've forgotten the way to get to the shelter of his knees. We've tried to heal and comfort ourselves, all on our own, but we really needed to be able to find this path again. To find it under the dead leaves. There are leaves on the path, you have to pick them up with your hands, one after the other, carefully, so that the moon doesn't scorch the slender path that leaps like a kid goat under the moon.

"And when we're close to him, in the streams of his saliva and in the wind of his words, he'll say to us:

"'My lovely little man, with your pretty little fingers that grab and squeeze, come here my man, let's see if you remember how to soothe things with your hands. That's what I taught you at the very beginning, when you were on my knees—a mere babe with your mouth full of my milk...'"

Suddenly, the grand vision gets all jumbled:

"...milk...mou...mouth...plain, wool, milk, milk, milk..."

Then a rattling and a grating, as though you were jamming on the brakes of a cart racing downhill.

In one bound, Jaume is there beside the bed.

Janet is twisted, his head buried in the pillow. A darkish fluid gurgles at the bottom of his open mouth. If he's going to die...

"Janet, Janet, hey!"

The eye, which had already been glancing back from beyond the land of the living, returns to earth, still trembling like a periwinkle tossed in the wind. He rallies, and his tongue rolls around:

"...milk, your mouth full of milk, and no blood yet on your hands."

Silence.

You can hear Marguerite snoring.

"It's over now," Janet says to Jaume, "get a grip on yourself."

When he went back to the ghost village to fetch water, Jaume found a woman's comb: one of the tortoiseshell kind that sticks into a bun. He found it under the mulberry bush, where the grass was flattened as though somebody lay down there regularly. Certain words spoken by Janet came back to his memory, as well as Maurras's remark. He put the comb into his pocket.

When he got home, even before he unhitched the mule, he went straight to his daughter's bedroom. He left the comb on the dresser, between the glass-domed clock and the wicker alms basket full of buttons.

He glanced around this room as though he expected it would reveal the secret life of his daughter: petticoats hanging on the wall, an old corset on a chair, a lace on the bedside rug. From a half-opened dresser drawer, the tail of a coarse, yellow chemise spills out. On the headboard, a pair of women's trousers is spread; a wide, oval slit gapes between the grey flannel thighs. An installment of a popular novel—*Chaste and Debased*—rests on the night table.

The comb is in a good spot. You can see it easily.

So now, this morning, Ulalie has been doing her hair in front of the mirror, and, naturally, she's stuck the comb in her bun. But on her way to the meadow she's come to a halt on the sunken pathway. In this spot, nobody can see you from any direction. She's taken hold of the comb and examined it front to back, turning it over between her fingers.

She's stood still for a long time, waiting for her thoughts to return from the place where she's just cast them.

Ulalie returns home. Jaume glances sideways at her bun. The comb is there.

"Is it you, father, who brought this?" she says, pulling the comb out of her hair.

"This what?"

"This comb!"

"This comb? No, what would make you expect—"

"I don't know. It was on my dresser. It's not mine."

"Then throw it away, if it's not yours."

"You can be sure I'm going to throw it away. What if it used to belong to a sick person? I wonder who could have put it on my dresser. I wasn't paying enough attention this morning when I was doing my hair."

And she throws the comb out the window.

And now, at noon, something happened as if by design. All of them were in the square, each one ready to take off on his own, since at this point they were as good as unconnected to each other. And all of a sudden, there it came, like a leaf the wind was trying to drag along the ground. All of them turned around together: It was the cat.

It crossed the little square in no hurry at all, just as though it was at home.

It was heading toward Gondran's house. Through the open window of the kitchen you could see Janet's bed and, in the middle of the bed, the mound that marked where Janet's body lay.

The cat has gathered itself into a ball, leapt onto the windowsill, and gone in.

This apparition of the cat has brought them together again, in fear.

Since the row broke out between Jaume and Maurras, all four of them have lived completely cut off from each other. Maurras would go and get water for himself, the others would go and get water for themselves, separately. Each of them would set off alone on the mountain trails, and then the water barrow would be brought back to only one house. And when the barrow was empty, you wouldn't ask for any water from your neighbor; you'd set off on your own again, along the mountain trails.

But this selfishness, while separating them from each other, has restored their concern for earth and put some distance between themselves and the overwhelming fear. They've been at the point of coming back to life.

Arbaud has been to look at the neglected grain fields. The over-ripe ears have buckled the stems, and thistles have erupted through the yellow mat. Patiently, with his sickle, he's cut a sheaf, happy to be alive and out in the open air, far from Babette's groaning and Marie's frightening body. Gondran, far removed from Janet, has picked a basket of grapes in his vineyard. There, too, it's nothing more than a vast republic of wasps, field mice, pillaging birds. On the village forge, Jaume has straightened out his ploughshare. The flailing of his arms and the rhythm of his hammer blows have, little by little, laid his anxiety to rest. Maurras, far removed from Jaume, has eaten fresh figs. "Tomorrow," he's been thinking, "I'll say to him: Let's make peace. I have a quick temper, but it's over. I'll go get water for everybody."

They were at the point of coming back to life, I tell you. It wouldn't have taken much. And then, the cat came. It came out from the mulberry bush, it strode out into the sunlight, it jumped onto Janet's windowsill. It didn't take more than five minutes altogether to get from the one place to the other, but at the same time, just like that, both earth and sky took on an ugly cast.

The cat reappears. From the windowsill it jumps onto the fig tree. The fig tree takes it up to the roof. It walks across the tiles. It heads toward Maurras's house. Fear has abruptly reunited Maurras with the rest of them. He's touched Jaume's arm.

"What do you say I bring it down?" And at once he's slipped the bandolier off his shoulder.

"No, leave it alone. Anything but that."

Maurras has obeyed.

From now on they're bound together, right to the bitter end. One by one the grains of wheat will sift through the matted stems, down to earth and the ants. Magpies will devour the grapes and the figs, and the coulter blade will rust in the autumn rains.

Now they're nothing more than one big, fearful body.

The cat has come back two or three times. It always comes out from under the mulberry bush. It walks on the tips of its claws, paws rigid, head held high. It passes by without seeing the men.

And then, another time, it shows up writhing, and its whiskers test the air, and its tapered ears seek out sound within the silence.

Or yet again, when you're securely locked inside your house, you suddenly see it appear on a windowsill.

This is what happened to Madelon Maurras. She'd gone to get some potatoes from the loft. She was picking them out from the pile and putting them into her apron. She wasn't moving too fast. When you're as old as she is . . .

You know what it's like, an attic? It's full of things that are as good as dead—old, broken-down armoires, worn-out shoes, blouses that have seen better days. All in all, things you've left there to die a quiet death. When you see them again, it's as though they're reproaching you. It's always a little sad.

On top of that, on this particular day the weather was gloomy.

She heard some plaster crack. She lifted her head: The cat was curled up in the frame of the skylight. It was licking its paws and cleaning one of its ears.

Ma Maurras dropped her potatoes and, quick as her old legs would carry her, she ran, lickety-split, downstairs to the kitchen. She swallowed a big draught of water to calm herself down.

Gagou's the only one who doesn't look scared. When the cat goes by, he laughs and bares his horsey teeth. Lips drooping, he lifts his wrinkled nose toward the creature. Sweetly he says to it "Ga gou, ga gou," sweetly and tenderly, with so much attention and tenderness that the strands of silken saliva ripple under his chin.

At the same time, something's bothering him, too. But what?

As soon as it's dark he comes out to prowl between the barricaded houses. For the first time, he alters his usual call. A muted whimpering leaks out of his mouth, like the moans of a lost dog.

He watches the windows of the bedrooms, where the shadows of women in their nightgowns, their hair loosened, pass by.

The lamps go out.

Gagou waits, motionless, in the dark.

This evening, just after nightfall, before people's eyes were used to the dark, Marie went into convulsions.

This happened all at once. Her mother heard her grinding her teeth. She touched her, and she could feel she was cold, rocked by big waves that made her bones creak.

Babette lets out a howl. Arbaud gropes in the shadows, looking for the lamp. At last he has it. But the glass globe rolls across the tablecloth and stops just short of the edge. He looks for his matches. No matches. Yes—here they are, at last. He strikes them so hard they don't light but merely score the darkness with a blue streak.

You can hear Marie's bones cracking. Babette moans, "Her head, Aphrodis, oh my, my, her head."

Finally, the lamp.

The little one is in her mother's arms. Within the space of a moment, between the last glimpse of daylight and the lighting of the lamps, both of them have become unrecognizable. Babette is nothing but two round, crazed eyes and a blackened mouth, like the mouth of a spring, ceaselessly moaning. Marie . . . Is this really Marie she holds in her arms? Or is it a gigantic heather root, full of knots, twisting and turning tortuously in a blaze? Two tiny, stiff hands claw at the shadows.

You can't hear anything but Arbaud's heavy breathing and the song-like modulations of the smoking lamp, as Babette fiercely kisses the heather root with her mouth wide open.

They've laid the girl down on her parents' double bed.

"Pull her legs apart, gently."

"Rub her with vinegar."

"Where is it—that vinegar?"

"There, on the mantelpiece."

"No it isn't."

"Yes."

"No."

"Yes."

"Ah, right, I've got it."

They fuss around the bed, run into each other, pull apart, hang on, stretch their hands out toward Marie, and moan.

They undress her. Papa tries to unbutton her little nightgown. The tiny, mother-of-pearl button slips out of his fingers, resists, pops back, dances, plays; then, in one swoop, he rips the gown open from top to bottom.

Her poor little body is exposed. And then it's like a storm breaks inside Babette:

Her Marie!

Pink like a rose she was, and plump, and now look what she's become!

Has she turned into this motionless thing you poke at, thrown down on her parents' bedspread?

The lamp sings.

They rub her sad, yellow flesh with lavender- and hyssop-scented vinegar. Her body relaxes. Her head rolls around on a softened neck. Her mouth opens, and you can see her teeth unclenching. One after another her delicate fingers stretch out, spread apart, and bend back to their usual position of a hand at rest. Now it's their Marie again, their flesh and blood, their two faces blended, their daughter restored.

"Lay her in her own bed," says Arbaud, "and put a warm stone at her feet. It's over."

He straightens his stocky frame. He takes two steps, and his broad hand moves toward the lamp. He adjusts the wick. The lamp quiets down.

"And what if it isn't true," Jaume thinks, all of a sudden. He's tried to accustom himself to Janet's view of the world, and the more he thinks about it, the more he has his doubts.

"What if it's just a lie to trick me, to take me in even further?"

He listens to the languid life of the trees around him, but it seems more hostile than friendly.

There's grass growing in the little square—tufts of yellow grass, same as on the hill. Their square's on its way to becoming part of the untamed hill again, the way it was before. The road to the flatlands is almost completely blocked by a huge, broken-down clematis. In a less unsettled time they would have quickly cleared the road. The world of trees and grasses is slyly attacking the Bastides.

"Tenderness! He said 'Tenderness.' Like it's that easy."

But if you don't go at it with your spade, if you don't go at it with your axe, if you don't clear a space around you, if you let the blade fall away from your hands just one time, then the whole mass of green surges over your feet and right up over your walls. It turns everything back into dust. Jaume raises his head. In front of him, on the other side of the square, a shadow slides into the shade of the oak: a wild boar! A wild boar out in broad daylight in the Bastides!

The beast barely conceals itself underneath the foliage. It's headed for the fountain. It sniffs the empty basin. It scratches at the ground with its hoof.

Jaume's rifle is right there against the wall. All he needs to do is reach out his hand. Jaume doesn't reach out his hand. This is something new and disturbing.

The wild boar has seen the man. Calmly, it chooses its resting spot and sprawls out in the dust. The rifle stays against the wall. Jaume, with his forehead thrust forward, his hands clasped between his knees, looks straight ahead as if he weren't seeing a thing. And the last thing he's thinking about is the gun. He's afraid. Fear has pierced him like a splinter, and his whole body hurts around it. He's afraid. That's why he hasn't stretched his hands out toward his gun. He's no longer thinking about his power as a human, he's thinking that he's afraid, and he's shrinking back inside his fear, like a nut into its shell.

The beast grunts as it rubs its back. It gets up, sniffs around, shakes itself heavily, and then, at an easy trot, takes off again into the woods.

It's a beautiful afternoon. The moon pebble rolls along the sands of the sky. At the same time, down toward Pierrevert, an odd, reddish mist is rising.

Jaume gets up. Over there at Gondran's the window is open. That white mound under the sheets, that's Janet.

"Aah, Janet, now I really see it—the harm that you do. It's right in front of me, like a mountain. You're on the other side of the barricades, with earth, trees, animals—all lined up against us. You're a dirty swine. My wife hanged herself up in the attic one night while I was out chasing hare. It was you who did that. Not with your hands, you can be sure, but with your tongue, your whore of a tongue. You have all the sweet taste of evil in your mouth..."

Jaume draws nearer. In front of the window, a fig tree forks into two twisted limbs. He climbs into the crotch. From here he can see inside the room.

Janet is stiff. His gaze threads through the shadows right to the wall where the post-office calendar hangs. He's mumbling in a low voice. Is he by himself?

No.

Next to him on the bed: the cat.

Someone's scrambling across the rocks on the hillside. Who? Maurras. Elbows tucked in, head lowered—driven by what? He's breathing so hard you can hear it from here.

As soon as he gets to the square he throws himself, screaming, at Jaume. But before he's able to speak, he stands there gesticulating, red in the face, streaming with sweat. And as soon as he opens his mouth he takes a gulp of air so huge that it chokes his words up inside him.

Finally he gets it out:

"Fire, fire..."

He stretches his arm toward the hill.

That mist they saw a few minutes ago, now it fills the sky. You can look at the sun right through it—round and ruddy as an apricot.

Jaume's moustache gives a twitch. He licks his finger and holds it up in the air: "The wind's coming from there, quick..."

They race from house to house, bang on doors with feet, hands, shoulders, yelling.

"Whoaaa, whoa, I'm here!" cries Arbaud as he tumbles downstairs, tying up his woolen belt. Gondran, Marguerite, Madelon, the valet, Ulalie, all of them burst out of their doorways in a rush of skirts and corduroys. Their faces are pocked by the heightened color of their eyes and the gaping pits of their mouths. Babette opens her bedroom window: "What's happening, what on earth is happening now?"

"The fire, the fire!"

Maurras is hopping up and down, between his mother and Gondran: "... it's swallowed up Hospitaliers woods, and farther, toward Les Collines, it's all over, burnt to the ground, nothing left. When I got up to the Espel heights and saw all of this ... ah me, good God, good God!"

"And Garidelle?"

"It's headed there."

"And Gaude?"

"It's burning it all up."

"Son of a whore!"

Jaume is holding back a little from the others. He's a bit off to the side, on his own. He feels himself growing tall and solid like a tree. All at once, his heart has been freed of dread. He listens to it beating, deep down inside himself, naked and exposed, beating away with its precious cargo of blood.

"Good, this time we know where it's coming from. We see it for what it is, and we know what we have to do. It could have been a lot worse. We're ready for it. I'm ready for it, yes, I am. Things are going well now, things go well from the moment you know what you're dealing with."

Really, the air is like an aromatic syrup that's been thickened with odors and heat.

Jaume reaches them in a single stride. With his right hand on Maurras's shoulder and his left on Gondran's, he stands between them, like a tree with sturdy branches: "All the children—out of here.

"Arbaud, get your little girl over to Gondran's. They'll put her in the back bedroom. Ulalie, go and help Babette. Ma Madelon, you go to Gondran's too. Everybody to Gondran's. Get going. Don't split up, so we'll know where you are if we need you. And on top of that, if you're all together you won't be afraid."

"Now for us: Arbaud, get your axe and your spade.

"Maurras—your spade, and your pitchfork too.

"Gondran—your axe, some rope, and your flail.

"And you, boy, you come with us. Run to the house, grab my two axes, the big one and the small one too. They're under the workbench."

The women run by.

"Babette, hey, Babette, watch out for the kid's blanket."

"Mother, get something to cover yourself with."

"Don't stand in the way there, kid, get a move on."

Windows open up:

"Father, did you take the key to the armoire?"

"Get going, get going, quick," says Jaume.

"Father, the key to the armoire . . . the key? . . . Father?"

"What?"

"The key to the armoire?"

"Behind the clock, behind the glass dome."

Doors bang:

"The axes, boy?"

"Can't find them."

"Under the workbench, like I told you, you little scoundrel . . ."

"Arbaud, have you got it all?"

"I've got my billhook too."

"I've got two pickaxes," says Maurras.

Gondran comes out of Les Monges.

"They've put Marie to bed."

"She didn't cry?"

"And my mother?"

"Gad almighty!" goes Jaume. "Are you ready, or not?"

A flock of birds, as thick as a river, flies crying overhead.

Jaume climbs into the crotch of the fig tree. In the room, Janet lies stiff, at rest, in the same position he was in a moment ago. Near him, the cat grooms itself with short strokes of its claws.

"Janet, it's blazing at Hospitaliers, do you hear me? The wind's coming from over there. Don't you have anything to say to me?"

A silence with a stream of wind roaring through it, loaded with violent essences. Then you hear Janet cry out with all his might:

"Jackass."

It had spread like hellfire and damnation down there, between two villages where people were burning the stalks and leaves of dried-up potato plants.

The slippery fire-devil leapt from the heather brush at the stroke of three in the morning. To begin with, it was raging in the thick of the pinewoods, making a hell of a racket. At first people believed they could master it before it did too much damage. But it roared so hard for the whole day and part of the following night that it wore out the arms and wearied the brains of all the lads who were fighting it. By daybreak, they saw it slithering its big body in between the hills, like a torrential stream, more robust and gleeful than ever. It was too late.

Since then it's thrust its scarlet head through woods and moors, followed by its flaming belly. Trailing behind, its tail beats at the embers and the ashes. The devil crawls, it leaps, it advances. Lashing one claw to the right, one to the left, it guts a whole oak grove on one side; on the other it devours twenty white oaks and three clumps of pines. Like a stinger, its tongue flicks into the wind to taste its direction. You'd think it knew where it was going.

And it's this sickening muzzle soaked with blood that Maurras has seen just below them in the combe.

Babette was scared to be in the back room, so they laid a mattress down in the kitchen for Marie and some sacks beside it for her mother and her baby sister. Between the back door and the sideboard they piled up big sheets of jute—the kind they used for wrapping up hay—for Madelon to sleep on.

"Don't worry about me," says Ulalie, "I'll find someplace easily enough."

"What a crowd!" exclaims Marguerite, "there's some comfort being all together."

The walls of the room toss her back and forth like a limp ball. She travels from the linen cupboard to the buffet. She'd like to give everybody sheets, to make coffee, at one and the same time, and she wanders around empty-handed, not knowing where to begin, and she laughs with a big laugh, frozen like in a photograph.

"Help yourselves, help yourselves. I don't know which way to turn anymore. Babette, get the cups, Ulalie, hand out the sheets, get out the flowered blanket, under there..."

They've lit the petrol lamp. Janet's bed raises the old man's body right to the edge of the shadow cast by the lampshade.

Twice already Marguerite has said: "Ulalie, come and lie down here behind the stove, you'll be comfortable here, you'll have a bit of space."

"Let me be. I have lots of time. I wouldn't be able to sleep, knowing they were just over there." When everything was arranged, the others bedded down on the floor on straw pallets. Now they're all stretched out, at rest: Babette between the two girls, Madelon in her corner between the sideboard and the door, fully dressed in her wraparound skirt and her scarves, Marguerite on the bedside rug. She's taken off her blouse, but left on her petticoat and hose. She's lain down flat on her back, and her ample breasts, covered with freckles, flop, one on one side, one on the other, projecting their thick, rose-coloured tips.

Long-drawn breaths have already merged into a chorus, interspersed by short puffs that flit through little Marie's feverish, dried-out lips. And through the twin notes that play through Marguerite's nostrils. And through the pipe-smoker's rattle issuing from old Madelon. Once in a while, a raucous gurgling rises up through this concert, swells, diminishes, ceases: Janet is breathing with difficulty.

They've trimmed the wick of the lamp. The light is a yellow ball fastened to the hoops of the iron hanger, a compact sphere stuck in the middle of the room, whose rays don't even reach into the corners. It barely brushes Babette's pretty, upturned white nose, one of Marguerite's breasts, and the hem of Madelon's petticoat.

Suddenly, the shadowy wall lights up, and a casserole dances against it in silhouette. The window opposite is lit up by a big, dazzling, russet flower.

Ulalie moves closer to the window.

"There, now it's grabbed hold of Les Ubacs," she murmurs to herself.

Outside: the blackened bulk of the empty houses and, beyond them, the hill brushing the belly of the night. The hill's contours are outlined by the russet flames devouring the woods of Les Ubacs, lower down on the neighbouring hill.

With its freight of plants and animals, the hill rises up, dark, massive, heavy with immobility and power.

"And if this hill gets roused up like the rest..."

The lamp gutters. The ball of light shrinks. Babette's nose—it's nothing more now than a tiny, pale triangle, anonymous. Only Marguerite's breast keeps its semblance of a breast, lifting and falling to the two tones of her snoring.

As she faces the window within the dark wooden interior, the glare of the blaze hollows out Ulalie's harsh features.

The lamp has just guttered out. Very quietly.

The breast, the nose, have faded. On the wall where the cooking pots hang, a big, reddish patch is flickering. At its center there's a little pattern, egg-shaped, which elongates, then flattens. When it's inflated it's the projection of a flaw in the glass through which the flames of Les Ubacs are glaring.

On the hearth, an ember groans for a moment, then goes out.

A cock crows. The oak shakes itself off in the wind. It must be dawn.

A dreary, grayish thread of dawn. The clock strikes seven. With firm finality.

Marguerite is the first to wake up. She sits on the bedside rug where she's slept and scrapes long and hard at her belly with her nails, as though it were the drum of a tambourine. She slips her breasts inside the straps of her chemise and then pushes them snugly into the bodice of her corset.

The door opens. Ulalie pokes her head into the opening. She seems put out to see Marguerite awake.

"You're already up?" Marguerite asks her.

"I couldn't sleep. You know what—Les Ubacs are completely on fire."

"Les Ubacs? . . ."

"Les Ubacs?" Marguerite asks, a second time. She's still half asleep, completely out on her feet. She can't come to grips with the fact that Les Ubacs are burning.

"What time is it?"

"Almost seven-thirty."

"Seven-thirty? But you can't see a thing!"

"Les Ubacs are on fire, that's why you can't see anything. There's so much smoke you can't see Sainte Roustagne anymore."

"Oh, my goodness, this time it's…" Marguerite says, terror-stricken.

Then, as though coming back to herself:

"I'm going to make coffee."

At the sound of the percolator, Babette wakes up all at once, with a cry and a defensive gesture.

"Hey, what's going on? I was frightened. Does it ever smell like something's burning."

"It's Les Ubacs that are burning," Marguerite says, casually, as she goes about serving the coffee.

Suddenly the door opens and slams back against the wall. The women turn around in unison: Jaume is standing on the threshold.

Silence. They hear a cup roll from the table, fall, and shatter.

"Oh, Jaume," goes Babette.

Ulalie comes forward and touches her father's face.

"What, what's the matter with me?"

One side of Jaume's walrus moustache is completely burned off. His eyes are gleaming in the midst of soot and sweat. He's lost his jacket; one sleeve of his shirt has been torn off, and you can see all of his sinewy arm, where tendons thick as fingers snake between tufts of white hair.

"And Aphrodis?"

"And Gondran?"

"They're all right, they're all right. I left them on the bank of the Neuf. Over there, it's gone out. I came to get coffee, brandy, bread, a bit of everything. If you still have some omelet left, wrap it up for me in a piece of paper. Give me a bit of ham too. Now it's taken off at Les Ubacs. That's bad—completely exposed to the wind. I caught sight of it on my way over. In the thick of all that smoke I didn't know where I was anymore. Let's hurry. I'm going back.

"No, no bottles. Where would you want me to put them? I don't want to have to carry them in my hands the whole way. Fill up the jug, stick the casserole lid on it, it's the right size. Don't go out. You have no idea where you're headed in these hills, it's catching everywhere. Stay here, stay together. Either Gondran or I will be back by dark."

He leans forward toward Marguerite and asks gently, "Your father? He hasn't said anything?"

Her full, flushed, moon-like face lifts up, with its pretty, round, blue eyes, blue like the spaces in the foliage of trees, and there's nothing behind them.

"No, why?"

When he's ready to leave, all harnessed up with shoulder bags and knapsacks, his jug, and his basket in hand, he changes his mind: "Ulalie, do you have your scissors? Cut this off for me," he says, pointing to the remaining half of his moustache, "it's bothering me."

Near the watering trough he runs across Gagou.

"Aah, you good-for-nothing, get moving!"

Gagou angles alongside him, on a slant, like a dog sidling up to a whip.

"Hey, don't be afraid. In the name of the devil! Here, carry this."

He hands him the water jug, and they take off.

And so, panting gleefully now in step with Jaume's elongated strides, Gagou has entered into the vengeful heart of the high country.

They follow the valley along the side of the slope. In every direction, the smoke is roiling and crackling. You can see the ground you're walking on for about fifty feet around, and for six feet above your head. But that's it. Beyond that, nothing but smoke.

As you walk along, a shrub looms here and there through the veil, passes, disappears. Now and then a panic-stricken bird plummets down, grazes the ground, flexes itself to get its strength back, and launches again into the murky mass that flows like a river in place of the sky.

Jaume is keeping an eye on the idiot.

"Hey, Gagou, don't go down, it's bad there, follow me—here."

He points to the spot just behind him, and Gagou obediently latches on to his heels.

Suddenly, a long knife of flame cuts through the smoke to their left. A pine thrashes wildly, crackles, twists, crashes down in a shower of sparks. One of them bursts into flame in the dry grass.

"Gagou, you son of a whore, give it everything you've got, let's climb up."

They tackle the hill on a slant. Three paces higher up, and they're engulfed in smoke. Completely. Jaume flings his hand back, grabs Gagou's arm on the fly, and pulls him along.

"Get a move on, kid."

It smells damnably of burning. You can hear the pinecones crackling and bursting. Could it be burning up ahead there, too?

Two large hares, as hard as rocks, hurtle in between Jaume's legs. Next thing you know, you hear them squeal down below, when they reach the knife edge of the flame.

Maurras stands alone on the hill. Alone beside a tall, robust, gleaming pine. The tree ruffles its dense, green plumage and sings. The trunk has arched itself into the prevailing wind...and then, with a strain, has raised its reddish arms, thrust its fine greenery into the sky, and stayed there. It sings mysteriously, in a low voice.

Maurras has looked at the pine, then at the smoke that's rising from the bushes below. He's done this instinctively, without reflection. He's said to himself: "Not that one. No, it won't get hold of that one."

And he's started to hack away around it.

In one fell swoop, earth has erupted in anger. The shrubs fought back for a moment, cursing, but then the flame reared up and crushed them under the soles of its bluish feet. It danced, the flame, crying with joy, but as it danced—the sly devil—it crept right down to the junipers, who were completely defenseless. In no time at all they were consumed, and they were still crying out while the flames, now out on flat, open ground, leapt across the grasses.

And now it's no longer a dancer. It's naked. Its reddened muscles are twisting. Its heavy breathing scorches a hole in the sky. You can hear the bones of the scrubland cracking under its feet.

Maurras hacks to the left and to the right, in front and behind, then takes a leap backward.

Suddenly, they're face to face—Maurras and the flame. There they are, dancing again, facing one another, jostling, backing up, rushing at one other, tearing each other apart, swearing...

"You goddamned gutless coward..."

And, out of the corner of his eye, Maurras checks on the gleaming pine.

But the flame's fighting like a trickster.

Flexing the backs of its thighs, it leaps as though it wants to let go of earth once and for all. Across its slender body, you can see the entire hill, scorched. It's already gotten into the pine and it's gutting it.

"Swine!" Maurras yells, and he jumps back into the smoke.

The ground falls away under his feet. He races at full tilt. In a flash, his spine becomes a fiery patch. The muzzle of the blaze pants after him. The flame leaps over the ridge. To his left the smoke settles, dense and motionless, like a circular stone. A shadow leaps out of it, coughing and spitting. Two curses.

"Jaume, it's you?"

"Hey, so it's burning up top too?"

"Everywhere. We've got to get a move on. The only gap left is Les Bournes."

Which means they're going to have to race for at least half a mile through the twists and turns of the choked valley.

It's no time for joking.

Jaume ditches his basket, makes sure he still has the bottle of brandy in his pocket, and heads off.

But what about Gagou?

In midflight, Jaume pulls up.

"Gagou, Gagou..."

Up above, the gleaming pine crashes down in a wonderland of sparks.

"Gagou..."

A bank of smoke collapses and rolls downwards.

Never mind...

In the end, he must have slipped away too. Jaume resumes his muscular, hunter's pace.

Out of the land of smoke, across the light-colored carpet of scrubland, three men are running. One of them is Maurras for sure—you can tell by the way he flings his feet out sideways.

The other two? Jaume hopes that Gagou is one them. No—it's Arbaud and Gondran. Even though it is the two of them who've returned, you have to hear them speak to recognize them. They have no more eyelashes, their skin is scorched, they can hardly breathe, their underwear is steaming, and they smell charred. The cuff of Arbaud's pant leg is fringed by a rim of sparks that are gnawing away at the fabric, thread by thread.

"Nothing to be done?"

"No. We sent the boy back home. It's too risky."

They climb, all four of them, up the Bastides' last defense: the foothill of Les Bournes, still intact, though flame is already licking at its base.

From the summit, the enormous extent of the burning woods reveals itself: A black carpet, scintillating all over with embers, stretches right across to the outskirts of a village that one had never been able to see when there were tall trees in between. It's gleaming now like a naked bone.

That's what one sees in one direction.

In the other, everything's still soft, ever so soft, covered with grasses and olive groves. There's a bowl-shaped depression, like the imprint of a woman's breast, in the grassland. In the middle sit the

Bastides, and near the houses, there's a little white patch that's moving—maybe Babette? Ulalie? Madelon? Marguerite? Or, maybe just Arbaud's youngest daughter, playing in the square.

The fire keeps climbing.

The four of them stand there watching it.

Down below, the woods are already crackling. The wind knifes between the walls of Lure and rends the smoke. The flame leaps like water in an uproar. The sky bears a heavy rain of glowing pine needles. Burning pinecones, clicking as they fly, score the smoke with blood-red streaks. A massive cloud of birds rises straight up toward the shrill reaches of the sky, gets drunk on the purer air, drops down, soars again, whirls around, cries. The terrifying suction of the blaze carries away whole wings, torn out and still bleeding, which swirl like dead leaves. A flood of smoke surges up, blots out the sky, wavers for a second in the wind, and then, flexing its sooty muscles, holds still and spreads. Inside its smoky flesh, birds crackle in agony.

Jaume is trembling from head to foot.

As though it was trying to shake off a bad dream, Maurras's gaze leaves the hollow of the Bastides and shifts over to Jaume, feels its way across Jaume's face, delves into his wrinkles, into his folds, under his eyes, around his mouth, looking for hope.

"And your moustache?"

"Phooey," goes Jaume, with a motion that means to say: "It's the same power that's destroying us and earth. My moustache? It's there . . . in the flames . . ."

Down below, the little girl plays on in the square of the Bastides.

"Let's go."

After he lost his grip on Jaume's jacket, Gagou ran frantically through the smoke. He was wailing with fright. Now all at once he's come to a standstill, wonderstruck and trembling with joy. A long strand of saliva drools from his lips.

The dense curtain has parted. Right in front of him, ten junipers are burning all at once. It's over quickly. The flame continues to leap skyward, but now it's like ten golden candelabras glittering. All the branches are glowing embers, even the twigs, even the fine netting of stems and veins in the leaves. They're still standing upright like living trees, but instead of dark, motionless wood they're fiery worms that undulate and twist, coil up, unwind with a light, clear, crackling sound. It's pretty.

"Ga, gou . . ."

He comes nearer, holds his hand out, and, in spite of the fire that's gripping his feet like a vise, he enters the land of a thousand golden candelabras.

The women weren't ready for this. It was far away, this fire, and now, all of a sudden, here they are, the men, tumbling down on top of them: "Hurry, cover up the windows with wet sheets, and everybody get inside." Next they set to hacking with all their might to open a ditch in front of the houses. Arbaud is slashing away at the dry grass and at the thatch of abandoned grain with big, rage-filled strokes of his scythe, off balance, as though he were drunk or crazed.

Babette is crying. Marguerite is sniffing back tears. Only Ulalie has disobeyed orders. She's gone back outside and now, along with the men, she's hacking at the grasses and the undergrowth with her sickle to help clear an open space in front of the Bastides.

Jaume looks like he has a hundred arms. The grayish, sticky air must be distorting appearances, because he looks gigantic and mobile, like a prehistoric lizard. He's everywhere at once: He pounds with his pickaxe, he runs, he yells out words that the rest can't understand but are glad to hear anyways.

"What a man!" thinks Maurras.

Yes, but if Jaume is battling with so much fury, the poor devil, he must have felt fear stirring deep within himself. In the midst of his activity he's able to forget about it.

As long as he was at a distance from the Bastides, he was battling only against the blaze. A blaze—it's something natural.

A short while ago, when he got back, the first thing he saw was

Janet's bedroom window, Janet's bed, and the white mound marking Janet's body.

Now he's seen into the heart of the matter. The crux, the hub of the relentless wheel is this little heap of bone and flesh: Janet. All at once he's seen earth's life-force spurting up all around him in leaps of hares, sprays of rabbits, flights of birds. Right under his feet, earth swarms with wild things. The clicking of grasshoppers raises a clatter, clouds of wasps whine and drone. Over there, spread-eagled over that decayed mushroom cap, a praying mantis darts its long, sawtoothed proboscis toward the flame. A crazed dung-beetle puffs its wings up against a tree trunk. Streams of worms ripple under the grass. Any kind of creature that knows anything at all is taking flight.

"Before long we'll be completely on our own. The whole hill has turned against us, the whole huge body of the hill. This hill that's curved like a yoke that's going to smash our heads. I see it. Now I see it. Now I know what I've been afraid of since this morning. Janet, hah, you dirty bastard, you've pulled it off."

A burst of anger straightens him up.

"And what about us now, don't we count?"

He grabs his flail. His fist tightens around the wooden handle. Power runs through his arm, in clearly defined ripples. Pins and needles run through his flesh.

He walks over the flame. Under his feet, the grass scorches.

"Ah, now I've found you out at last, you rotten swine."

He strikes at the hill with his big flail. The flame shrinks back around him. A black patch smokes where the boxwood flail-head lands.

"Dirty good for nothing."

The blows ring out. It looks like the bruised and battered hill is finally going to be defeated.

"Jaume, Jaume! . . ."

Maurras is running after him, grabs him by the shoulders, shakes him as if he's trying to bring him back to his senses:

"Are you crazy? You mean you can't see it?"

The time has come: the cunning flame has spun its opponent around. In another moment it will be closing its gaping, gold-toothed maw around him.

In one bound Jaume gets clear.

"Light the backfire."

Ah, the lighting of the fire that's our friend, not our foe. It's ready to take off from our feet, crouching over the ground like a warrior preparing to charge. Look: It strangles our enemy, knocks it down, smothers it.

But ah, what rotten luck, now both fires are raging together and turning back on top of us.

A terrible rumbling makes the sky shudder. The earth monster is awakening. It's making its massive, granite limbs grind to the very center of heaven.

Maurras throws his pickaxe to the ground and takes off on the run.

Arbaud's scythe rings out as he hurls it full force onto the stones.

A door bangs. Windows crash down.

Behind all the uproar, the cries of women.

"Father, father…"

The leaves of the big oak are crackling.

So, is the whole world really falling to pieces?

Jaume, his legs worn out, his head sagging, collapses.

"You dirty whore!" he says as he falls. He pounds fiercely at the hill with his bare fists.

Honestly, he thought he was dead. He had glimpses of brimstone and cypresses.

He lay stretched out on his back, short of breath. The air, avoiding his lips, passed by his mouth like a wall. All the little life-bearing packets were dancing on the frantic currents of his blood. Big swirls of blood were stirring up sprawling seaweed: his wife, hanged in front of the attic skylight with a triangle of dawn planted on her wine-dark face; the movement of his daughter's lips, so, so petite, ever so petite, when she mouthed "Papa" for the first time. Then a mass of smoke came pouring down on top of him and he thought: "It's all over."

Afterward, suddenly: silence and sunlight. And now he's found himself alive.

He wasn't altogether certain of it. For a moment it seemed to him that death had hardly changed him at all, but then, right away, he realized he wasn't really dead.

He's gotten back up on his feet and he's checked on the Bastides. They're still standing. The oak is a bit singed. And the roof of one of the outbuildings is still smoking. But it's sure to go out by itself.

In the blink of an eye, he figures out what's happened: A tongue of the backfire, propelled by the main mass of the flames, must have leaped across the open ground and rushed down on top of the houses. The main river of fire, that did get diverted all the same, is now flowing away to the left of them.

They are saved.

Ulalie runs across the square. It's still swamped in smoke. Only half her body emerges out of it.

"Nothing to worry about, father?"

"No, daughter."

Maurras, laughing, with all his teeth bared, shouts out:

"It's heading down the other side toward Pierrevert. We're safe."

"And once it's over there, who cares," says Arbaud, "it's nothing but stones, it'll do what it wants to. We're done with it."

Marguerite comes out of Les Monges. She's wearing a red camisole with white polka dots, the underarms stained with sweat. With her flat feet and her big, fur-lined slippers, she walks as if she were pulling her legs out of two feet of mud. She comes toward them, preceded by the aroma of hot oil.

"I've made a bacon omelet," she says.

They've eaten, all the men together, at Gondran's. And every one of them has unbuttoned his trousers.

"Me, old buddy, I was in a fine pickle—it was catching here, it was catching there, it was crackling under my feet..."

"I kept scratching myself and scratching, then it turned out my shirt was on fire and scorching my back."

"A pinecone in the face, yep, they explode like gunshots. I got hit by a pinecone right in the face, I'm telling you, right there beside my eye..."

All of this spoken with arms waving and enough pounding on the table to make the glasses jump. Arbaud hugs Babette. He leaves black streaks on her forehead and her cheeks. He's determined to bring a glass of wine and a biscuit to their little Marie, who's stretched out on her mattress. From under the bedclothes, she slips out a wrist as thin as thread, and the spidery tips of her fingers tremble as she grasps the glass.

"It can't do her any harm today."

This was a golden day. The wine had never tasted so good, nor the omelet, nor the tobacco.

"You're a cook fit for any establishment," Gondran says, as he gives Marguerite an affectionate pat on the bum.

Only Jaume holds back from the merriment, with a dense band of shadow across his brows.

Doubtless, like the others, he can feel the warm, fragrant caress of renewed life brushing like petals across his skin, but there's an uneasiness still embedded in his bitter heart.

Before coming in, he took a glance at the whole of the Bastides. They had their usual look—four houses crouched under the oak. But the fields!

Yes, they've fought, they've won, but the blows of the other side have hit hard.

From where he sits, he looks over at Janet's bed, and sees Janet like a tree trunk, under the sheets.

A moment ago they tried to get the old man to drink, and he played possum. When Marguerite insisted, he turned his head away, dismissively. Now he's just opened his eyes. From his bed, his glance, clear and hard as a knife, has slid over toward the men.

"We won," says Jaume.

"We won. That's all well and good.

"What it cost us, we'll find that out soon enough. It cost a lot, I'm afraid, an awful lot, but we won.

"We're all still here, in one piece...but...

"But all of us are still here because it was over in the very nick of time.

"In the very nick of time. A tiny bit longer and we'd have been done for. Another ten minutes, I'd have been dead, and the Bastides would have been done for. It was a near miss.

"All in all, it's another strike against us, like the spring, like the row with Maurras, like this disgusting business with Ulalie that I've had on my mind ever since, like Marie's sickness.

"We won again, up against this last blow, but it was harder.

"And it tore off a piece of our hide.

"We won again this time, but what about the next strike?

"The hill.

"It's always there, the hill.

"And Janet? He's always there.

"We're in a shaky state. If the hill hammers a little harder now...

"It will always be there, the hill, with its enormous power to harm us. It can't go away. It can't be defeated once and for all.

"This time we won. Tomorrow, the hill will win.

"It's just a matter of time. What will we have accomplished after all, in the final reckoning? We'll have held out a little longer—that's all.

"This time it let us go, barely, but it spared us. Tomorrow it will hammer us good and hard.

"And who knows, maybe it won't wait until tomorrow.

"Maybe it's already flexing its muscles to put us away, in one fell swoop, for all eternity, before we've even had our first sip of morning coffee.

"There's nothing to be done. The hill would have to forget about us. And then we'd have to live together like we always have, as good neighbors, as good friends, not doing each other any harm.

"But as long as Janet's around…

"The dirty bastard.

"It's Janet who made this happen, with his head full of ideas.

"Things were going well before all of this. It had never said or done anything to harm us. It was a good hill. It knew pleasant songs. It hummed like a big wasp. It let us have our way with it. We never dug too deep. One or two blows of a spade, what harm could that do? We walked across it without fear. When it spoke to us, it was like a spring. It spoke to us through its cool springs and its pine trees.

"He must have messed with it.

"He must have known this whore of a secret—to be able to control it, to have it at his beck and call, to stir it up whenever he wanted.

"It had to be this stinking bastard who knew it.

"He doesn't even have two bits worth of life left and he's still making mischief.

"He doesn't want to go out by himself. He wants us all to go along with him—women, trees, chickens, goats, mules, everybody and everything—like a king…

"For sure he wants to make the rest of us cross over to the other side with him, all together.

"And his life's hanging by a thread.

"We can't afford to give him the time."

"Alexandre, give me your cup," Marguerite says as she comes forward with the percolator.

"I won't give him the time," thinks Jaume, his head fit to burst with rage.

After the coffee, the brandy. The little bottle that Jaume has lugged around in his pocket all morning sits on the table.

Gondran jokes as he pours it out: "If this had been milk you'd have churned it into butter."

Then a blissful silence; matches strike; somebody bangs a pipe against the table.

This is an hour opening up in flower, like a meadow in April.

All of a sudden, Jaume stands. They watch him. He's uneasy. Babette doesn't dare to keep on soaking her lump of sugar.

"All you men, we have to go outside. I have something to say to you. It's serious."

They can tell it's serious by the look on his face. Behind his unshaven beard his cheeks are as white as candle wax.

"All right, let's go."

They stand up, ill at ease and listless. They won't gladly give up the spring daisies that were flowering just a moment ago.

"Let's go under the oak. The women don't need to hear everything. We'll tell them what we want to, nothing more."

"Is something the matter?" asks Gondran.

"Yes, there is something the matter," says Jaume, pointing past the Bastides at the earth, naked, scarred, blackened, wisps of smoke still trailing across it.

"Let's sit down. This is going to take a while.

"I didn't want to tell you this back there for a number of reasons. First, because of the women, and second, for another reason that you'll understand later.

"It's been a while that I've been thinking about it in this way, without really knowing for sure. Now I do know, and I'm going to tell you.

"But first, because it's a deadly serious business that I'm going to talk to you about—serious for me and for you too, whether we agree about it or not—I want to know if you trust me. I mean, whether when I ask you for something, you believe I'm asking you because it's the right thing, and for the good of us all?"

Jaume has been looking mainly at Maurras.

"Me, I believe it," goes Maurras.

He's sincere—it's obvious.

"You've never done any harm," say the others.

Jaume is getting paler and paler.

"I've never done any harm, that's for sure. I've been mistaken, like everybody else, but that...that's not my fault. This time I'm not mistaken. I'm sure of what I'm going to say to you. Remember this: I'm sure of it. I don't need to talk to you about what happened last night and this morning. If I told you that we'd barely escaped, we'd agree, wouldn't we? But don't you believe that this fire is just one more vicious trick, like the others we've suffered through lately?"

"What do you mean?"

"Yes, you do remember. We were sitting pretty just a few months ago. Things were coming along just so, the grain was doing well, we were getting by very nicely with what we had in our barrels, in our crocks, in our jars. I'd already had a word with the broker in Pertuis about my beans, and the prices were good. Things were falling into place.

"Then, all at once, it started. If I remember right, it began on the day when Gondran came to tell us that Janet was raving. We came over to your place and we listened. It made me feel peculiar. The rest of you too. You must remember, we talked about it that evening on the way home. Next there was that business of Gondran's, with his olive grove making groaning sounds down in the bottomlands. It was already starting to smell a little worse. After that came the cat. Since then there's been the spring, Marie, the fire...The spring, we found a way around that. The little one, she doesn't look like she's getting any worse—isn't that true, Arbaud?—but she's not getting any better either. The fire—we don't know the full story yet.

"When I saw the cat, I didn't hide anything from you. I said: 'Keep a sharp eye out on every slope,' but in all honesty, I didn't believe it could get this bad. And now—and I've thought hard about this—if, after the spring, after Marie's sickness, after the fire, there's still another dirty trick that comes down on top of us, then what will we do?"

"..."

"We've been pretty well rattled."

"..."

"To be blunt, if one of these days a trick as dirty as the one that just got played comes down on our heads, we'll be done for. That's my opinion."

"Mine too," says Arbaud.

"And here's the worst of it: If these were all natural happenings, we could cope. You can't have bad luck all the time, you get through it, but—do you want me to say it? All of this is being done to harm us, us and our families, the Bastides, you name it. And by someone stronger than we are."

"Who?"

Jaume looks at Gondran.

"Ja...net," Jaume says slowly.

"He is a bit nasty, the old bastard, it's true," says Maurras.

Not a peep from Gondran.

"If I say it's Janet, it's that I know, it's that I'm sure of it. I'm not a man to wrong anyone else for nothing. Remember—everything I've said, everything I'm going to say, these are things I'm sure of. I've dug up the proofs, I've weighed all of it up inside myself, and I'm sure of it."

Gondran coughs.

"What is it that makes you say you're so sure about it?" he breathes. "I don't have any doubts about you, I have confidence in you, but to say you *know*? Can't we look for a minute at whether I've thought about this too?"

"Listen," Jaume goes on. "It was when the spring failed. After we'd been tramping through the bush searching for the underground stream and we came home that evening completely wiped out. All that night I couldn't stop chewing it over. It seemed unbelievable to me that we hadn't found anything. This country around Lure is brimming with water, but for us it had turned into a kind of burning flesh. I got the idea that from the other side of the air we know, and from inside earth, somebody else's will was coming at us head on, that these two wills had locked horns, like two goats who have it in for each other. Right was on our side. We were looking for answers as best we could, we couldn't have done any different. So, why was the other one so headstrong?

"In the morning I went to see Janet. He's the oldest—so I thought he might know something useful. And he did. He boasted about it, but he didn't want to tell me. When I couldn't cure Marie I took it on myself to come and talk to Janet again. I didn't do it willingly, you can be sure of that. He'd already done me a dirty turn. This time he showed his true colors. You can't have the remotest idea of the things he said to me. I saw his malice standing right in front of me, like another man. He told me we were all going to croak, and that this made him glad, that he was doing everything necessary for it to happen. I tried to make him listen to reason, I got angry, but there was nothing to be done. And then it was he started to talk, as if he himself had been the source of the mystery. It all took shape—a whole world being born out of his words. He conjured up countries, hills, rivers, trees, wild animals. It was like his words were marching ahead, stirring up all the dust of the world. Everything was dancing and spinning like a wheel. It totally dazed me. In a glance, I saw, as plain as day, how all earths and heavens are one, including this earth where we exist—but transformed, totally varnished, totally oiled, totally slippery with malice and evil. Where before I used to see a tree, a hill—in other words, all the things we're used to seeing— there was still a tree, still a hill, but I was seeing right through to the terror of their essence. Power in the green branches, power in the clay-red folds of earth, hatred that mounts up in the green streams of sap, and hatred that trembles in the wounds of the furrows. And then I saw someone holding a thorn in his hand, who was ripping open the wounds to heighten the anger."

They were listening, with their eyes wide open, their jaws slack, their lips drooping, their pupils dilated, their hands frozen, overwhelmed by this vision of the avenging spirits of the vegetal world.

"I've seen it move—the hill," Gondran murmurs.

"And it's Janet who's holding the thorn," concludes Jaume. The sweat is running down his ashen forehead.

"The slimy bastard," goes Arbaud.

"Thank goodness we have you on our side," says Maurras.

A silence falls. Since the fire, the silence is even heavier than before. The trees can no longer keep it hoisted above people's heads. It crushes earth with all its weight. Then, from the very heart of the blackened plain, the howling of a dog keens skywards.

"And so?"

"And so, it's him, there's no question about it."

"Janet?"

Gondran bites his hand, this massive hand that's utterly useless in the face of this dilemma. He finally takes it away from his mouth, in order to be able get his thoughts out.

"It is true, I wasn't saying anything, but I'd figured it out. Not the way you tell it—you're quicker than we are—but I had my suspicions. You're right, it's from Janet that it's coming, but there's nothing we can do about it."

"Yes there is."

"What?"

In back of Jaume's lip they catch sight of a yellowed tooth; it disappears.

"We have to kill him," he says.

Ideas like this don't sink in immediately.

"Good god!" goes Arbaud, once he's understood.

Now that the overwhelming fact is out in the open, Jaume breathes easier. Suddenly he's gotten all red in the face. Bulging veins wrap around his temples, like the roots of an oak. He speaks in a voice drained of enthusiasm, a voice that barely escapes his mouth before the words drop down at his feet. And, at the very core of what he's saying, he embodies his idea, like a wooden statue of a saint in his woolen mantle.

"We have to kill him, it's the only way. He may already be scheming what it would take to kill us—the rest of us. It comes down to knowing whether or not we want to live, whether we want to save Babette, the kids, the Bastides. This is the only chance we have left to defend ourselves. We've battled against the hill's body. Now we have to crush its head. As long as its head's still raised up, we won't be free from the threat of being destroyed."

"He's a human being," says Gondran.

"He's not human," says Jaume. "Not a man like you, me, the rest of us—we have respect for life. We live our lives the same way we carry a lantern that the wind's trying to blow out—we shelter it with our hand, and we're humble in the face of life. Lots of times you've picked up newborn chicks, ever so nice and warm, and they nestle into your palm? When they're in there, right in there, between your fingers, if you squeezed just a little you'd crush them. We've never even been tempted to do that, because we're men. Him, it's not chicks he has in his palm, it's us. And we've already felt him tightening his grip, and we know that he has every intention of tightening it right to the limit. He's not a man."

"Hey, listen I'm not contradicting you," continues Gondran softly, "I know it, I haven't lived with him for twenty-five years without getting to know all about him. I do agree with you, it's from him that everything's coming and . . . we would have to kill him, as you say, if we wanted to pull ourselves out of this, but he's almost down to his last breath. We might not have to wait long before it happens by itself . . ."

"And if you wait," Jaume flings back, "if you wait, he'll make you suffer as long as he has even an ounce of life left. The closer he is to the end, the more nasty he'll get. When you come right down to it, if we wait, we'll all end up crossing to the next world at one and the same time, with him out in front and the rest of us bringing up the rear, like a bunch of penitents on the march. What does he have to lose?"

"You're right," says Gondran. "But what I've been saying, it's because he's my father-in-law. You understand? And on top of that, maybe I ought to talk about it with Marguerite first."

"Go find her. We have to put an end to this by tonight."

Gondran has just gone in to Les Monges.

Jaume looks at Arbaud and Maurras.

"It's just as well we sort this out once and for all," he says.

And the two others have answered at once, firmly:

"Yes, for sure." And then, "*Basta.*"

With Marguerite, it was settled quickly.

When Gondran stepped in to Les Monges, the other three men felt suddenly afraid of her. They saw her flying over the grasslands, her nails thrust forwards, crying full blast. Jaume had thought of every counter-argument: "I'll say to her: 'So, now you want that all of this should go back to being bush again?' I'll say to her..."

No, with Marguerite he didn't have to say anything. It was settled quickly. She's come out staggering, stamping down on the grass, and now she's over there wailing, crouched against the watering trough.

They've gone some distance away from her to settle the matter.

"You're the only one who can do it," Jaume says in a whisper to Gondran, "he won't suspect you."

"With what?"

"With your hands. In the state he's in, it won't take much."

"Right here," says Maurras, pointing to the nape of his neck. "I was a butcher in the regiment, and I know what I'm talking about. Right here, like you do it with rabbits. One sharp blow, and then you hold the pillow over his face."

"Show me," Gondran asks.

Maurras lowers his head and gets Gondran to feel his spinal cord. "Right here, with the edge of your hand."

"Will he bleed?"

"No, not if you hit sharply. Maybe a drop, but don't pay any attention, put the pillow over his head and press down on it for a minute."

A silence, with the four men motionless. In an instant, Gondran makes up his mind: He takes a first step, the hardest one, then he heads off, a solid mass, his back hunched, his arms stiff, his hands held away from his body, as though he's afraid he'd stain his trousers with them. With each step, he looks like he's trying to make sure that the earth is solid too.

In the gray evening, a vulture from Lure glides overhead, its talons open wide.

A cry. The door bangs, and Babette comes running out, trailing her shawl.

"He's dead, Janet's dead! Come quick!"

Old Madelon appears on the terrace. Gently, without showing much emotion, she makes a sign: "Come."

Gondran had been on the very verge of going into Les Monges. He jumps back to get himself well away from the door, to make it abundantly clear that there was nothing afoot, that he didn't actually go in, that Janet has died of natural causes, pure and simple.

Babette is over there, under the oak. She's mouthing explanations and making motions that loosen her hair from its bun. She's putting it up again as she babbles on, and suddenly, Gondran is moved by the arc of her beautiful, raised arms. Life washes over him like a huge, roaring wave. His ears are full of music, and he drops down heavily to the ground, like a drunkard.

It's true, Janet is dead.

They've taken off their hats. Jaume has set his pipe on the side-board, but since it's still smoking a little, he goes outside to tap it out, taking care to muffle the sound. Marguerite is sniffing back quick, tearless sobs.

"Gritte, we have to get him dressed while he's still warm. He'll be too stiff afterward. Bring us his Sunday jacket."

So that Gondran and Maurras can pull on Janet's corduroy trou-sers, Jaume has taken hold of the corpse under the armpits, and its limp head lolls back onto his shoulder.

They've laid him out on the bed and bound his jaw with a white scarf.

"Gritte, close the shutters. Light a taper. We men will keep vigil over him. You women, go on to bed."

Gondran digs around in one of the dresser drawers. He's looking for a pipe.

"D'you have any tobacco left?" he asks Arbaud.

Night has fallen, dense and sombre. Down below, toward Man-osque, the blaze is still burning a little. A cricket is singing on the terrace.

Gondran, straddling a chair, his eyes shut, is pulling gently on his pipe.

And Janet continues to gaze at the post-office calendar.

They remained there like that, saying nothing, smoking away, until almost eleven o'clock at night. Then, just as the last stroke sounded from the mantel clock, Jaume raised his hand and said: "Listen."

Outside, from the depths of the shadows, a sound.

They've asked themselves: The wind? The rain maybe? Whatever it is, it's brought a cold sweat to their brows.

They've gone to open the door. They've cocked their ears. . . . And they've all had the same idea: "Get the lantern."

They've gone out. There wasn't anymore doubt about it, but they wanted to make sure by seeing it and touching it.

The fountain is running.

Maurras looks over toward the doorway of Les Monges, from which the yellowish light of the funerary candles is seeping. He touches Jaume's arm:

"Hey," he says, "that was just in the nick of time."

They've waited the obligatory twenty-four hours, and this evening they've buried Janet, at the edge of the land that was left unscathed by the inferno.

It's Maurras who's made the casket, and it's Babette who's read a passage from her missal, over the grave.

On the way back to the Bastides, Gondran has said to Jaume:

"You should go to Manosque tomorrow to do the formalities. Monsieur Vincent will make out the certificate for you, and then you'll have to go to the town hall."

"I'll go, but not till tomorrow afternoon. I'll walk down as far as Les Plaines, and I'll take the Banon post. What do you have to say about it, Ulalie?"

They've gone back to their place. Something mysterious is worrying Ulalie. She's pacing around the table, gazing at the window, which is full of night and stars.

"Do as you like."

Even so, he's gotten up at six o'clock this morning. It's no small deal to go to Manosque. You have to bring out your good clothes, unfold them, sweep off the mothballs, find a neckerchief, brush your hat, polish your shoes, shave . . .

While he's lathering up his soap with crystal-clear water from the fountain, he thinks about that morning, not long ago, when Gondran shaved with wine. Now there are six good feet of earth piled up over Janet, and the spring has come back to life. Just in the nick of time, like Maurras said. Jaume has had enough, he's weary. He's lost weight. He thinks about flowers, about hayfields in flower, and how the women call out to each other while they're forking over the hay.

"Hey, Jaume!" shouts Arbaud from below.

Jaume hasn't really snapped out of it yet—he jumped up right away, but then, while he was opening the window he saw—there behind the oak—the low mound of freshly dug earth the length of a man...

"Later..."

"I've come from Bournes vale. Somebody's dead over there. It must be Gagou."

Ah, yes, nobody had thought about Gagou for the past two days.

"He's all shriveled up like a baby cicada. I'm certain it's him. I took a quick look at his face. The rats have eaten off his nose. I recognized him from his buck tooth. I'm going to tell Gondran."

Gagou! So, it's not over after all! There's still this thing lingering in Jaume's brain, those words of Janet's. They haven't died out yet, those words.

But, ah, since we're already having to deal with things that hurt, we might as well get this one over with too, right away. Suffer a little, and then be sadder but wiser.

He turns his attention back to his shaving.

Ulalie comes in, carrying the water jug.

And, as he continues to lather the soap across his face:

"You know what, Ulalie, Arbaud's just seen Gagou. He's dead. Completely burned up. Down below, at Bournes. The rats have eaten off his nose."

"I know, I heard."

She leaves the jug under the sink.

He looks at her in the mirror as he goes on stroking the brush over his days-old beard.

"Where is it you say he's at?" she asks.

"At Bournes."

She goes into the corner where the tools are kept. She digs into the pile of implements and pulls out the new spade.

In the mirror, he follows all her movements.

She touches the tip of the spade, then goes to the door. Jaume turns around. He tries to turn slowly. He tries to speak clearly. But it's only a muted whisper that makes it through the foam: "Where are you off to?"

"Where it is you say he's at," says Ulalie, repeating her words.

They look at each other eye to eye, face to face. And, imperceptibly, Ulalie loses control of her facial expression. A crease deepens next to her mouth, fills out again. Her eyelids tremble.... She pulls gently on the door and heads downhill.

So, it is really true?

Janet's six feet under and there's already rot inside his mouth, but the words he sowed go on multiplying like weeds.

"Ah, you should have a last, good laugh, you dirty bastard. You've had me again all the same. For the rest of my life I get to chew on this bitter herb, over and over again."

Suddenly, an enticing desire to abandon himself to the winds of fate takes hold of Jaume, as though a whirlwind were grabbing him by the waist and bearing him away.

A little rest! Rest, with warm doorways where you can soak up the sunshine and smoke a pipe!

Ulalie has come back.

Jaume is set. He's clean-shaven, and a cotton neckerchief, loosely knotted, lets his rosy, pointed Adam's apple show through. His corduroy jacket is still creased from the armoire. On the chair beside him lie his light-colored, wide-brimmed felt hat and his walking stick.

She's come back. It's around half past twelve.

Before returning to the house, she carefully scraped her spade with a bit of flat stone, to make the dirt fall off.

Her father is sitting at the table, alone, before a plate of ham and a pitcher of wine.

She goes over to the corner of the shed where the tools are kept, replaces the spade, wipes her hands on her apron, and turns around.

She wears her usual expression. Except that her upper lip is hanging over her lower lip. In such a way that the narrow opening of her mouth is completely covered up.

"There's no soup?" says Jaume.

"No, I didn't have time."

She sits down near the table, her hands on her knees, and says nothing.

"You aren't eating?"

"I'm not hungry."

She's painfully gulping back a thick layer of saliva. Heavy thoughts are weighing down her head.

And all at once, after a long silence, she says in a weak, plaintive voice, as if she were talking to herself:

"And me, what am I going to do now?"

He looks at her: his daughter! The Lili who used to run around under the apple trees in her white bonnet. She is truly homely, but behind her reddened lids, her eyes gleam like shattered coal.

What she said is true, though. Will she always have to labor, without ever knowing the joys of womanhood?

It's time to go. Jaume gets up.

"Ulalie," he says, "listen: We could take on a lad from the public assistance. Sixteen years old. They're already full-grown men, and you can get them to do whatever you like, you know?"

They're sitting, Jaume and Gondran, on the rim of the fountain basin. They're drinking absinthe. The bottle is bobbing in the cool water. It's dusk, the hour of ice-blue stars.

"It's good, our water."

Lure's shadow covers up half of the earth. From the houses come the sounds of dishes and the melody of a child's lullaby.

"Aphrodis is sending his youngest to Pertuis, to her grandmother's, for a change of scene."

"She looks like she's doing better."

"Yes, like everything else."

"Oh, you know what, we're keeping the cat. It comes from the Grandes Bastides. You remember when Chabassut brought me that load of hay? It must have gone to sleep inside it, by the looks of it. It's his cat. It's pretty bold. It's a good little critter. It catches rats—you should see it."

"Haven't you started your ploughing yet, Alexandre?"

"Tomorrow."

The metallic smell of watercress wafts from rivulets that the fountain is once again filling. The spring sings a long lament that conjures up cold stones and shadows. The watering trough quivers, teeming with life.

Suddenly, Jaume leans over and sets his glass down in the grass.

"Look," he says in a low voice.

On the slope, toward the wasteland, a black shape is moving. A wild boar.

"Ah, son of a whore!"

Jaume has already grabbed his gun and shouldered it. He takes double aim, steadily, with deadly intent. The shot rips through the familiar sounds of the fountain and of the houses.

"He's done for."

"Hey, hey," Arbaud yells from the fields.

"Hey," Maurras yells from the olive grove.

They run, all four of them, toward the wild beast that's making clods of earth fly as it writhes in agony.

It's a fat, young boar, with bristles like a green chestnut. The buckshot has disemboweled it, and its blood gurgles out between its thighs. It tries to stand up again on its hooves and it howls, laying its big, white, burrowing teeth bare.

And it's Maurras who finishes it off, with some blows from his billhook.

They've skinned it while it's still warm, and they've shared out the meat generously. And the men have washed their hands in the trough of clear water. Jaume has kept the skin for himself. He's stretched it across two willow sticks, and he's hung it from the lowest branch of the oak for the dew to soften it.

Now it's night. The light has just faded from the last window. A large star keeps watch over Lure.

From the skin, which turns in the night wind and drones like a drum, tears of dark blood weep in the grass.

ACKNOWLEDGMENTS

THIS TRANSLATION has been a labor of love and the focus of my creative life for a number of years. Without the involvement of many others, it would never have come to fruition.

In particular, I'd like to thank Jacques Mény, president of the Association les Amis de Jean Giono, for his unwavering encouragement and support; Edmund White, for his warm appreciation; Wendell Block, for his insight; the late Walter Redfern, for his generosity; Edwin Frank and Susan Barba of NYRB, for their vision and commitment; and Debbie Honickman, my fellow traveler, for her acumen, and for the beauty of her art.

—PAUL EPRILE
Creemore, Ontario, 2015

TITLES IN SERIES

For a complete list of titles, visit www.nyrb.com or write to:
Catalog Requests, NYRB, 435 Hudson Street, New York, NY 10014

J.R. ACKERLEY Hindoo Holiday*
J.R. ACKERLEY My Dog Tulip*
J.R. ACKERLEY My Father and Myself*
J.R. ACKERLEY We Think the World of You*
HENRY ADAMS The Jeffersonian Transformation
RENATA ADLER Pitch Dark*
RENATA ADLER Speedboat*
AESCHYLUS Prometheus Bound; translated by Joel Agee*
CÉLESTE ALBARET Monsieur Proust
DANTE ALIGHIERI The Inferno
DANTE ALIGHIERI The New Life
KINGSLEY AMIS The Alteration*
KINGSLEY AMIS Dear Illusion: Collected Stories*
KINGSLEY AMIS Ending Up*
KINGSLEY AMIS Girl, 20*
KINGSLEY AMIS The Green Man*
KINGSLEY AMIS Lucky Jim*
KINGSLEY AMIS The Old Devils*
KINGSLEY AMIS One Fat Englishman*
KINGSLEY AMIS Take a Girl Like You*
ROBERTO ARLT The Seven Madmen*
WILLIAM ATTAWAY Blood on the Forge
W.H. AUDEN (EDITOR) The Living Thoughts of Kierkegaard
W.H. AUDEN W.H. Auden's Book of Light Verse
ERICH AUERBACH Dante: Poet of the Secular World
DOROTHY BAKER Cassandra at the Wedding*
DOROTHY BAKER Young Man with a Horn*
J.A. BAKER The Peregrine
S. JOSEPHINE BAKER Fighting for Life*
HONORÉ DE BALZAC The Human Comedy: Selected Stories*
HONORÉ DE BALZAC The Unknown Masterpiece *and* Gambara*
SYBILLE BEDFORD A Legacy*
MAX BEERBOHM The Prince of Minor Writers: The Selected Essays of Max Beerbohm*
MAX BEERBOHM Seven Men
STEPHEN BENATAR Wish Her Safe at Home*
FRANS G. BENGTSSON The Long Ships*
ALEXANDER BERKMAN Prison Memoirs of an Anarchist
GEORGES BERNANOS Mouchette
MIRON BIAŁOSZEWSKI A Memoir of the Warsaw Uprising*
ADOLFO BIOY CASARES Asleep in the Sun
ADOLFO BIOY CASARES The Invention of Morel
EVE BABITZ Eve's Hollywood*
CAROLINE BLACKWOOD Corrigan*
CAROLINE BLACKWOOD Great Granny Webster*
RONALD BLYTHE Akenfield: Portrait of an English Village*
NICOLAS BOUVIER The Way of the World
EMMANUEL BOVE Henri Duchemin and His Shadows*

* *Also available as an electronic book.*